WOLF AT THE WINDOW

Suddenly, Mandy began to feel uncomfortable. It was as if someone were watching her. Glancing around the room, her gaze was drawn to the window. Mandy felt her body go rigid and held her breath. It was there! The wolf was there! It was staring right at her!

This time it couldn't possibly be her imagination. The wolf was enormous — Mandy could see its great mane of white fur shining in the moonlight. And its gaze was so intense that it seemed to bore right into her. She stared back at the wolf, not daring to look away for an instant, in case it disappeared.

Read more spooky Animal Ark™ Hauntings tales

Wolf at the Window

Ben M. Baglio

Illustrations by Ann Baum

Cover illustration by
John Butler

SCHOLASTIC INC.

New York Toronto London Auckland Sydney
Mexico City New Delhi Hong Kong Buenos Aires

Special thanks to Tanis Jordan.
Thanks also to C. J. Hall,
B. Vet. Med., M. R. C. V. S., for reviewing
the veterinary information contained in this book.

ISBN 0-439-44896-4

22 21 20 19 18 17 16 15   8 9 10/0

Printed in the U.S.A.   40

First Scholastic printing, October 2002

HAUNTINGS

One

"Hurry up and close the door," Adam Hope joked as Mandy Hope and her friend James Hunter struggled in, carrying between them a big basket of logs and putting it by the fireplace. "You're letting in all the cold."

"And all the heat out," Emily Hope added, looking up from her book and winking at her husband.

"Is *that* all the thanks we get?" Mandy asked, sitting down and pulling off her rubber boots. She pretended to sound indignant. "It's freezing out there *and* it's starting to snow."

"It's coming down in really big flakes," James said, "and they're beginning to stick."

1

"All the more reason to get the logs, then," said Mandy's dad. "Anyway, you two are young and energetic. Mom and I are old and tired."

"I don't think *I'm* old, Adam," Mandy's mom said, raising her eyebrows and looking sideways at her husband. "I'll certainly agree with the 'tired' part, though. I don't think we've ever been quite so busy as in the last few weeks. It seems like we've treated nearly every animal in Yorkshire!"

"That's because you're the best vets around," Mandy told them with a grin. "Everyone wants to come to Animal Ark." Animal Ark was the Hopes' thriving veterinary practice in the Yorkshire village of Welford.

"Not this weekend, I hope," Dr. Emily said, raising her eyebrows. "We don't want Simon and Alistair snowed under with work." Simon was the nurse at the clinic. He and Alistair King, the on-call vet, were holding down the fort while the Hopes were away in Scotland.

"I think we might be snowed under instead," Dr. Adam observed, looking out of the window.

The birthday invitation from Dr. Adam's old college friend had arrived last month. Angus Mudie was celebrating his fortieth birthday with a huge party. Mandy had been really excited since the invitation included her and a friend.

"Turn it over and read the back," Dr. Adam had suggested.

"Why not come up to the majestic Scottish Highlands and stay a few days to unwind?" Mandy had read aloud. *"You can see the wildlife park that I helped set up."* She looked at her dad, eyes shining with anticipation. "Dad, can we go? Can I take James?"

"I don't see why not," Emily's dad had responded. "Mom and I could use a break."

Of course, Blackie, James's Labrador, would come, too. While most of the other guests would stay in the main house, which was split into modern apartments with kitchens, the Hopes had taken advantage of the peace and quiet of the old gamekeeper's lodge.

Now, after a long drive, they were relaxing beside a roaring log fire in the cozy living room. The lodge was a solid building, made from thick blocks of stone, with a big oak door. Though it had been modernized, it still had the original furniture, with paintings all around the rooms. The front door opened into the hall and the back door went into the kitchen, where there was a wood-burning stove that heated the house. Someone from the main house had come in and lit the fire and put fresh sheets on the beds before they'd arrived. Angus had even left a welcome basket for them in the kitchen.

Mandy's parents' bedroom was full of pictures of birds. Two tiny bedrooms had been built in what had once been a loft.

"Where can Blackie sleep?" James asked in a worried voice when they carried up their bags and Mandy pushed open the doors.

"Hmm," Mandy said as she studied the tiny rooms. "If we move your night table and push the bed against the wall, he could just fit." Together they heaved the bed against the wall and made a space for Blackie.

Mandy's and James's bedrooms were reached by a steep, winding staircase in the middle of the house. These rooms had small square windows that creaked open sideways, but the downstairs windows were larger and made of several panes of glass. They were set in the stone and couldn't be opened at all.

Dr. Adam settled back comfortably in his chair. "This is the life." He sighed. "Now, if *someone* would make us a nice cup of tea, everything would be just fine," he said, looking pointedly at Mandy.

"OK," Mandy said. "I can take a hint, Dad."

"Your dad says that he's hungry, too," James told Mandy as he joined her in the kitchen. "So am I, actually."

"When *aren't* you hungry, James?" Mandy teased, laughing as James turned pink.

"When I'm asleep?" offered James.

"Right," Mandy said. "Let's see what's in here." She opened the wicker basket Angus had left.

"Wow!" said James, his eyes lighting up.

There was a loaf of crusty bread, a huge slab of butter, half a dozen little jars of assorted jams and marmalades, a box of shortbread, and a packet that said, GENUINE SCOTTISH OATCAKES!

Mandy made a pot of tea, poured some milk into a jug, and set them both on a tray with four mugs.

"Will you take the tray, please, James?" she asked. "I'll look for some plates."

"OK," said James, picking up the tray.

Mandy held the door open for him, and James crossed the hall, heading for the living room. She had just turned back into the kitchen when the light started to flicker and then went out completely, plunging the kitchen into darkness. Almost immediately Mandy heard a crash. James must have dropped the tray.

Mandy stood still and tried to get her bearings in the dark. It was pitch-black, too dark to see her hand in front of her face. *It was probably just a power failure*, she thought. Perhaps they happened quite often here. She remembered that there were candles in most of the rooms.

Mandy stood very still and gradually became aware

of a noise. She held her breath. In the dead silence, she could hear a faint gulping sound that seemed to be coming toward her. She wasn't alone. There was someone or *something* in the room with her.

She gripped the table hard and tried to stop the shivers that were running up and down her spine. She could feel her heart pounding — it felt like it was in her throat. She tried to convince herself that old houses made strange noises. Something touched her foot. Slowly and carefully, she bent down to feel what it was. Her hand came in contact with cold, clammy skin.

"Aaaagh!" Mandy yelled loudly. She almost fell over backward as the creature leaped away. At that moment, the lights came back on and Dr. Emily charged into the room, followed by James.

"What happened, Mandy?" she asked in a worried voice. "We heard you scream."

"I don't know," Mandy said, making a face. "Something was on my foot and, when I touched it, it jumped up. Its skin was all rough and sort of bumpy."

Dr. Adam was standing in the doorway holding the tray of dishes and trying to look innocent. "I think you've just met Mr. Buffo," he told Mandy. "He's a rather large toad that lives under the sink. He's been there for years. Angus mentioned him when I phoned to accept the invitation. I forgot to tell you."

"I bet you did, Dad!" Mandy said.

James went over to the sink and moved the checked curtain that hung around its base. Sitting contentedly on the bottom shelf next to a bottle of floor cleaner was a very big toad. It blinked at them reproachfully.

"He's really pretty!" said Mandy. "Look at his amber eyes."

"I don't think you can describe a toad as pretty," James pointed out.

"Handsome, more likely," Dr. Adam said as he put the tray on the table. "Only one mug broke, but we'll need some more tea, please. And look what I found by the fireplace!" He held up a fork with a long handle. "It's a toasting fork. Why don't I slice that loaf and we can toast some bread in front of the fire?"

Soon a delicious smell of toast filled the air. They tried the oatcakes, too, with butter and jam on them, and almost finished the shortbread.

"If I can find some real oatmeal in that kitchen," Dr. Adam said as Mandy took his empty plate away, "I'll make us some real Scottish oatmeal in the morning. If I remember correctly, you have to soak it overnight."

"I noticed that Angus has left some salmon in the fridge," Dr. Emily told her husband. "The label says that it was smoked on the Mudie Estate."

"Would it have been caught in the lake?" James asked, giving an involuntary shiver. "I bet it's deep."

"Loch," Dr. Adam told him. "Lakes are called lochs in Scotland, and it certainly would be deep and cold. Angus used to say that it was often too cold to swim in, even in summer. Welford seems positively warm by comparison to the Mudie Estate," he added. "Speaking of which, would you put another log on the fire, please, James? And to answer your question about the fish, they could well have come out of the loch. It's a seawater loch, even though we're quite a way inland."

James dropped a log on the fire, sending sparks flashing up the chimney and into the hearth. Blackie, who had been curled up on the rug in front of the fire, leaped up excitedly, snapping at the fiery flying lights.

"Look out, Blackie!" Mandy called as she and James lunged to grab the dog. But they were too late. With a soft sizzle a spark landed directly on Blackie's wet black nose. He yelped in surprise and ran straight behind a sofa.

"Oh, Blackie, you poor thing," Mandy said when she and James got down on all fours to examine Blackie's nose.

"Let me have a look," Dr. Emily said, quickly putting down her book and standing up. "I hope the sparks didn't get in his eyes."

"Come on, Blackie, come out," James said, pulling gently at the dog's collar.

Mandy tried to help, but Blackie resisted all their efforts to coax him out from behind the sofa.

"It's no good. He won't budge," James told Dr. Emily.

"Let me have a look at him," Dr. Emily said, kneeling down in their place and looking behind the sofa. "Hmm, he'll be fine in a couple of days. It probably stung at the time, which is why he yelped," she told them. "His eyes are OK — no problems there." She ruffled the top of Blackie's head, and he looked up at them all sheepishly.

"It's his pride that's hurt more than anything," Dr. Emily said with a smile. "He's embarrassed! I bet we won't see Blackie curled up in front of the fire for at least half an hour."

Mandy smiled to herself as she watched James kneel down and whisper something softly in Blackie's ear. As soon as they'd arrived earlier that afternoon, she and James had taken Blackie to explore the estate. The lodge was high on a sloping bank above the loch, surrounded by pine and oak forests. Hills covered with mauve heather stood in the distance. Mandy, James, and Blackie had come back when the snow had started to fall.

Now, Mandy looked out the window to see if it had stopped snowing, but all she could see was the reflection of her dad and his reading lamp. She moved closer and shielded her eyes with her hands to block out the light. In the moonlight, Mandy could see that although it was no longer snowing, a light dusting of white flakes covered everything.

Suddenly, as she leaned closer, she spotted a pattern etched in the glass. She moved nearer, noticing that the etching seemed to be of an animal.

As her eyes grew accustomed to the darkness outside the window, she began to make out the shape of the etching. It was an old dog — it looked like a German shepherd. The Mudie family must really love animals to have a picture of a dog etched in the window. But as she watched, she became puzzled. The dog's eyes looked so real, and they even seemed to be yellow. How had they done that? Suddenly, the whole picture in the window seemed to slip into a different focus. Mandy took a sharp breath.

It's not a picture, Mandy thought with a jolt. *It's a* real *dog! There's a dog outside the window — it's looking in.*

Mandy's first urge was to run outside to bring the dog inside. But she couldn't move. The animal's eyes held her. They bored into hers — it was almost as if they were trying to tell her something.

For what seemed like ages Mandy stood mesmerized. Then questions slowly formed in her mind. All of her experience with dogs told her that they didn't *have* yellow eyes. But this one did. And its head was really big — this dog must be enormous!

The creature's neck was so large and its coat so dense that there were rolls of fur around its neck, which looked like ruffs. Its fur was white, flecked with gray, and there was a dark gray stripe like a T across its forehead and down its muzzle.

Mandy wanted to turn around to call the others to look, but she still felt rooted to the spot.

Suddenly, the creature stood up. As soon as it was upright and Mandy saw its long legs, she knew. It was a wolf. She felt a shiver start at the nape of her neck and slide down her spine.

Two

"Mandy?" Dr. Adam called urgently. "What's wrong? You're as white as a sheet."

Mandy signaled him to come, but her dad was already out of his chair and on his way across the room toward her. She put her finger to her lips and silently mouthed the word *wolf*.

Dr. Emily and James looked out of the window with worried faces. But when Mandy turned back to the snowy scene, the wolf was gone. She stepped forward and rubbed the pane of glass with her arm, trying to see if she could spot the creature walking away.

"It *was* there, honestly," she said, staring out anxiously. "It was a big gray-and-white wolf with yellow eyes. I was watching it for ages. At first, I thought it was a dog but, when it stood up, its legs were too long. And it was *huge* — its head was at least this big." Mandy held her hands apart to demonstrate the size.

Dr. Emily put her hand on Mandy's forehead. "You *are* very pale, Mandy," she said. "Are you feeling OK?"

"Mom, I *did* see it," Mandy said in a serious voice. She pressed her face against the cold glass of the window, but everything outside was still.

"Sometimes our imagination plays tricks on us, Mandy," Dr. Adam said gently. "Especially when we're tired. It's been a very long day."

Mandy squared her shoulders and looked up at her dad. "I didn't imagine it, Dad. I *know* I saw it."

"We would see tracks, wouldn't we?" James asked eagerly. "Surely it would have left tracks?"

Mandy shot him a grateful look. At least James seemed to believe her. She dashed to the door, undid the bolt, and pulled it open. Blackie sprang up and bounded to the door, his blister forgotten.

"Whoa there, Blackie," James said, grabbing his collar. "I think you should stay inside if there's a wolf around."

Mandy saw her parents exchange glances. She looked on the ground beyond the doorstep. There *were* some tracks there. But when Mandy followed the tracks with her eyes, she realized that they led to the woodpile.

"They're the footprints we made earlier," James said softly, coming to stand beside her.

Mandy made her way carefully to the outside of the window where she'd seen the wolf. There wasn't a single mark on the snow-covered ground. She couldn't believe it. She touched the window. It was dry. There was no mark where the wolf's breath would have clouded the cold glass. She looked at the patch of ground where the wolf had stood. It was covered by crisp new snow.

Mandy felt her dad's hands on her shoulders and looked up at him. "Face it, honey," he said, giving her a lopsided grin. "There haven't been any wolves in Scotland for hundreds of years. It must have been a trick of the light, maybe a reflection from the lamps, or something. These things happen."

"But, Dad, that's what I saw first, the lamp's reflection. That's why . . ." Mandy broke off. She looked from one to the other. She could see from their faces that they thought she'd imagined it, and she didn't know how to convince them. She took a deep breath and sighed. "OK, maybe you're right," she admitted grudgingly. But in her heart of hearts, Mandy *knew* that she'd just seen a wolf.

"Let Blackie out to run a little now, and then I suggest an early night would do us all good," Dr. Emily said in a cheerful voice. "I'm exhausted." She stifled a yawn and pushed open the front door of their vacation home. Blackie was snuffling impatiently at the door and rushed out, almost knocking Mandy's mom over in the process.

"Sorry," James apologized and quickly threw a stick for Blackie. Mandy giggled as James's dog hurtled after the stick, leaping up in the air with excitement.

"You've got so much energy, Blackie." Mandy laughed when the Labrador dropped the stick at James's feet.

When James threw the stick again, Mandy threw him another stick from the woodpile. Confused, Blackie skidded to a halt, then dashed after Mandy's stick.

Mandy grinned and then quickly looked back at the window. There was absolutely nothing to be seen. If an animal had been there, she realized with a shudder, it had left no trace at all.

"I think that's tired him out," James said, coming to stand beside Mandy. She heard Blackie panting as he ran up to them. But instead of bringing James the stick, the dog stopped and dropped it a short distance away from them, his tail firmly between his legs. No amount of coaxing from James could make him come any

closer. "He can be so stubborn," James said, shaking his head. "Let's go in — he'll follow us."

Sure enough, when they reached the front door, Blackie ran up to them, wagging his tail.

"You silly dog," James said fondly, rubbing Blackie's ears. "When will you learn to behave?"

Maybe Blackie wasn't silly at all, Mandy thought later as she climbed the stairs to her bedroom. What if Blackie had sensed something outside? She knew that dogs' hearing was really sensitive. She yawned and climbed into bed. Before she had had a chance to think about the wolf again, she was sound asleep.

The next morning, Mandy woke up early to find that the snow had melted. A milky-white mist hung over the loch, lit by the first weak rays of the rising sun. It looked warmer than yesterday but, when Mandy flung open the window, she was met with a blast of cold air. She hurried to close it again, and there was a sudden movement among the trees on the other side of the loch.

Vivid memories of the wolf came flooding into Mandy's head, and she froze as the mist swirled and cleared for a moment to reveal a figure in a blue warm-up suit, bent over with his hands on his knees. Mandy grinned. Her dad was out jogging. She quickly pulled on some warm clothes and gently opened James's door.

James was asleep, but Blackie opened one eye and looked at her.

"Come, Blackie," Mandy urged. "Let's go and find my dad." She ran downstairs, pulled on her rubber boots, grabbed her coat, and dashed outside with Blackie close at her heels. Sunlight was glinting on the loch as the mist shimmered away to nothing, and the cold, crisp air was full of birdsong.

Mandy glanced at the window where the wolf had been. Everything looked perfectly normal. *Could* she have imagined it? She had to admit that the wolf seemed unbelievable in the bright daylight. Mandy sighed to herself and ran around the loch toward her dad.

As Blackie went tearing past, Dr. Adam turned around and jogged backward. "Morning, honey," he greeted her, his breath puffing out like clouds of steam.

"Don't you think you might be overdoing it, Dad?" Mandy said, looking with concern at her dad's red face.

"I — *puff* — wanted — *puff* — to work up — *puff* — an appetite," Dr. Adam said as he slowed to a walk. "Wait till you taste some real oatmeal!" He laid an arm across Mandy's shoulders and gave her a little hug. "How do you feel this morning?"

"I'm fine, Dad." Mandy smiled at him. "Last night I was sure that I'd seen a wolf, but this morning, well . . ."

she broke off and bit her lip. "*Something* was there, Dad, honestly."

"Maybe there was, Mandy, maybe there was. After all, we don't know much about the history of this place," Dr. Adam said, looking at her thoughtfully as they reached the lodge and went inside. "Anyway, let me loose in that kitchen. Breakfast will be ready as soon as I've jumped in the shower!"

When Mandy and James sat down at the table ten minutes later, it was set with three bowls. A large pot of oatmeal bubbled gently on the stove.

Dr. Adam placed a large, steaming bowl in front of Mandy. "Sometimes, people dip the ladle in cream before serving," he said, filling a bowl for James, whose face lit up instantly.

"Mmmm," murmured James.

"Sorry, we're out of cream. But we do have salt!" He laughed, passing Mandy the saltshaker. "This makes it taste *really* nice."

Mandy's mouth fell open. "Ugh, that sounds horrible," she said.

"James?" Dr. Adam looked at James, who was blushing.

"Don't tease them, Adam," Dr. Emily said from the doorway. She was smiling as she came into the room, her red hair still damp from the shower and curling in tendrils around her face. She reached up into a cabinet and passed James a bowl of sugar.

"I think I'll stick with this for now," James said, relieved when he tasted the oatmeal. "This is delicious, Dr. Adam."

"Why, thank you, James," Dr. Adam said, putting a towel over his arm and making a small bow. "Compliments of the chef."

"Speaking of food, would you mind going to the store for me?" Dr. Emily asked Mandy and James when she sat down. "I brought some food with us, but we need milk and fruit, and maybe you could get some yogurt."

Mandy nodded. "No problem," she agreed cheerfully.

While Dr. Adam ate his smoked salmon and Mandy and James cleaned up, Dr. Emily sat at the table writing out a shopping list. "You should be able to get everything at the mini-supermarket we saw yesterday," she told them.

"I'll take Blackie," James said to Mandy, "but I'd better keep him on his leash if we're walking by the road."

With James holding firmly on to Blackie's leash, they set off for the village. Before long, the estate was behind them and a lonely road lay ahead.

The only vehicle to pass them on the way was a large green farm van with bales of hay sticking out through the back doors. When they arrived at the store, it was parked outside.

Piled up near the entrance to the mini-supermarket were bags of coal and bundles of logs and kindling. Three propane cylinders were roped together and tied to a metal ring attached to the wall. James tied Blackie's leash to the ring and told him to behave.

Inside the store, Mandy took charge. "If you get a basket, James, I'll find what we need," she suggested. She'd found milk, cheese, and some locally made yogurt and was just picking out some fruit when she heard raised voices.

"And I say it's all *wrong*!" a man's voice said loudly. "They'll be nothing but trouble, you mark my words."

Another man agreed. "He's right. They don't belong here."

"These outsiders and their stupid ideas . . . They should mind their own business," someone else added.

Mandy and James exchanged glances. "Do you think they're talking about us?" James whispered in alarm.

"Why should they?" Mandy said, her voice indignant. "We haven't done anything wrong. Now what else is on the list? OK, where are the magazines?"

A huddle of people surrounded the magazine rack. A man wearing blue overalls and muddy boots was talking furiously and shaking his fist. His face was deep red with anger and the veins in his neck were pulsing. He banged his fist down on the counter, making Mandy and James jump and the cash register rattle.

"*I* won't put up with it," he said, scowling. "And nor will any farmer around here worth his salt, not when they read this." He held a newspaper open to show the other customers the headline.

Mandy realized that he was standing right in front of the magazine she wanted and she stepped forward. "Excuse me," she said politely, trying to squeeze past him.

"It's nonsense!" a tall man said. He was smartly dressed in a green jacket and brown corduroy trousers. "What about my deer? They'll be after them next. Not to mention the game birds."

The man in the blue overalls whacked the newspaper, tearing the page. Mandy wondered what could have made him so angry. She looked at James, who was picking out a computer magazine and trying to keep a low profile.

"Let me say one thing," the man said in such a menacing voice that Mandy went cold. "There won't be wolves in Scotland while I live and breathe. You can be sure of that."

Wolves! Mandy could hardly believe her ears.

"Brett, don't you think you're taking it too much to

heart?" said the storekeeper as he weighed some carrots. "They're only young wolves and they'll be safe enough in the park. Angus and Duncan wouldn't do anything foolish."

"Foolish!" Brett spat out the word. Mandy decided that his narrowed eyes looked really shifty. The man rolled the paper in his hand and held it like a club in front of him. "It was a dark day when they brought wolves back to these parts, I'm telling you. They may be young now, but they'll grow and then what, huh? Those wolves will be trouble!" And with that he marched out of the store and slammed the door.

"Brett McCatter has always been a hothead," the storekeeper said to the man in the corduroy trousers.

"He has a point," the man answered. "It's troubling for any rancher in the area. Wolves are natural-born killers. I don't know what Mudie is thinking."

"What about the *bairns*?" a woman with a shawl over her coat said. "It's said that in the old days, wolves would take a *bairn* if they could."

Another woman nodded agreement. "That's true."

Gradually, the people drifted away, muttering to one another as they left the store, until only Mandy and James remained.

Mandy felt thoroughly confused. She couldn't figure

out what everyone was so worked up about, but it was definitely to do with wolves.

"Good morning! And what can I do for you?" the storekeeper asked Mandy kindly. "You're not from around these parts, are you?"

"We're from Yorkshire," Mandy told him. "We're staying in the gamekeeper's lodge on the Mudie Estate."

"Then you'll be up for the *ceilidh*," he said. "It'll be a big to-do." He laughed at Mandy's frown. "The birthday party, I mean. There'll be a lot of dancing going on!"

"Oh, yes," Mandy agreed. "But could you tell us what everyone was saying about wolves, please?"

"Don't worry your head about wolves," said the storekeeper, tsk-tsking. "They're not going to bother anyone." He shook his head before continuing. "Some people get themselves all worked up over nothing and they stir everyone else up while they're doing it. Brett is always trying to cause trouble, one way or another."

"But what's a *bairn*?" James asked. "The lady said that a wolf took one."

The storekeeper laughed. "A *bairn* is a child, and some say that wolves would carry them away. But that's an old wives' tale. You shouldn't listen to that nonsense. What's happened is that the wildlife park has just accepted delivery of two young wolves."

"Is that the wildlife park that Mr. Mudie helped set up?" Mandy asked.

"Yes. And some of the local people are getting very worried about their livestock. *Not* that there's any need to worry, in my opinion," he said, taking the basket from James and beginning to add up the items. "Duncan knows well enough how to keep his animals safely in their enclosures. They won't escape. All this talk of reintroducing the wolves into Scotland is jumping the gun. It's wrong for the newspapers to get everyone annoyed."

He handed James the shopping bag. "That's four pounds seventy. Thank you very much," he said, taking the money Mandy offered. "Why don't you go to the park and see the wolves? They're nice-looking creatures," he added as they left the store.

Mandy was thoughtful when they got Blackie and walked down the road. Suddenly, she stopped. "Wait, James," she said. "I'll just be a minute." She turned and ran back to the shop, but it was empty. "Excuse me," she called urgently from the door.

"Have you forgotten something?" the storekeeper asked, appearing from behind a beaded curtain that hung across a doorway.

"No, nothing," said Mandy, her voice unsure. "It's just that you did say *young* wolves, didn't you?"

"Yes, I did. They're not tiny pups, mind you — I think they call them juveniles," he said.

"And there used to be wolves in Scotland?"

"Yes, there were," the storekeeper answered. "More than enough. In the old days, the highlands were rich in lots of wildlife that you don't see today."

"Thank you," Mandy said as she closed the door. She couldn't help thinking of the huge, grizzled old wolf at the window, staring at her with its glowing amber eyes.

Three

Mandy had been lost in thought since they'd left the store.

"What's up?" James asked as they walked back along the road, with Blackie tugging at his leash.

"It's hard to explain," Mandy began. "It's just that, well, don't you think it's strange that I saw a wolf last night and today we find out that there actually *are* wolves near here?"

"Yes, but these are *real* ones," said James, turning to look at Mandy.

Mandy stopped dead in her tracks and stared at

James. "You think I imagined it, too, don't you?" she said, her voice full of disappointment.

"No!" James said hesitantly. "It just seems a little weird." He shifted uncomfortably. "No one else saw it — the wolf, I mean — and there weren't any tracks. There aren't any wolves around here, anyway, except in the park — we'd have heard if one had escaped."

"OK," Mandy said cautiously. "Anyway, I suppose the wolf that I saw wasn't that young. It was huge and its eyes were old and sad."

James opened his mouth to say something, then closed it again when Mandy gave him a look.

"And," she continued, "who says that *all* the wolves in Scotland have disappeared? What if some survived and are living in the middle of the highlands, where nobody knows about them?" Mandy was warming to her theory now. "And what if one came to the window last night and I happened to see it!" she finished triumphantly, setting off again toward the lodge.

"It's possible, I suppose," James said, looking doubtful. He knew better than to dismiss Mandy's idea. "But why?" he asked carefully, almost jogging to keep up with her. "I mean, why would it come and stare in the window?"

"Well, I don't know *why*," Mandy argued. "But it did! I *wish* I knew more about wolves."

"That's easy," James said, delighted to be on safer ground with Mandy. "We can look it up! There must be a library somewhere around here."

"Yes, there is," Mandy replied, nodding. "I'm sure I saw a sign in the village."

"Then we can find out all we want to know about wolves there. Let's take the groceries back to the lodge and then go and investigate," James suggested.

"Right," Mandy agreed, feeling much happier. "I'll race you up the driveway."

"That's not fair," James grumbled good-naturedly. "I'm carrying all the bags. You have Blackie and he loves to run!"

Mandy was out of breath when she reached the path that led from the main house to the lodge. She let Blackie off his leash and, while he darted in and out among the trees, she sat on a log and waited for James.

"That wasn't fair," James gasped, dropping down beside her on the log. He pointed to the shopping bags. "Where's Bla —"

Before James could finish his sentence, there was a huge commotion behind them. A rubber ball came bouncing down the path, closely followed by an excited Blackie. When he saw James, he didn't seem sure whether he should stop or go after the ball. James jumped up to grab him but Blackie was going too fast, and they both ended up in a crumpled heap on the ground.

Mandy was still laughing when a boy who looked about twelve years old appeared around a bend in the path. Blackie ran to the boy and sat at his feet.

"He's a good-looking dog," the boy said politely. "Is he yours?"

"No." Mandy chuckled, pointing at James. "*That's* Blackie's owner!"

The boy looked quizzically at James, who was sitting, disheveled, on the ground.

"He's mine," James confirmed, pushing his glasses back on his nose. "And he gets a little . . ." He searched for a word. "Exuberant!" he exclaimed.

"Exactly!" Mandy agreed.

"I'm Cameron Mudie," the boy said. "And you two must be Mandy and James!"

"That's right," Mandy responded. "And this is Blackie."

"We've already met in the woods," Cameron said. "I made him chase a ball."

"Do you have a dog, too?" Mandy asked him.

"I do, and she loves chasing that ball," Cameron told them. "She's very old now, and it's the only way I can get her to exercise."

"She's not a big German shepherd, is she?" Mandy asked cautiously.

"No way," Cameron said with a laugh. "She's a little brown mongrel called Beattie. Why?"

"Mandy thought she saw one last night," James said.

Cameron bent down and petted Blackie with a thoughtful look on his face. "I can't think of anyone around here with a German shepherd. A farmer farther north used to have one, but it was just a puppy," he said as Blackie rolled over onto his back. "Anyway, he's moved away. Maybe you saw something else."

"It probably *was* something else," Mandy said dismissively. She was beginning to think that she *had* imagined it. "What's the library like in the village?" she asked him.

"It's really good, actually," Cameron told them. "I've used it a lot while I've been researching a project about the history of our house for school."

"Really?" said Mandy.

"I've been doing it on my computer. Tell you what, why don't you both come over and I'll show you?" Cameron suggested. "I'll show you around the house, too."

"Thanks," Mandy replied, picking up the bag, "but we'd better get these groceries back and then we need to go to the library." She could see that Cameron was dying to know why they so urgently needed to visit a library, but he was too polite to ask.

"How about tomorrow, then?" he asked. "The library closes a little earlier this afternoon, but you've still got plenty of time. It's down in the village near the church. Nice to meet you both, and you, too, Blackie," he added, patting James's dog before walking away.

When they reached the lodge, Dr. Adam was outside, splitting logs from the woodpile for the fire. James grabbed Blackie to stop him from getting in the way.

"Hello, you two." Dr. Adam stood up and leaned on the ax. "You were gone a long time."

"We bumped into Cameron," Mandy told him. "He asked us to come over to the house tomorrow."

"He's got a computer," James added.

"Right up your alley, James," Dr. Adam said knowingly.

"We'd like to go back to the village to have a look around, Dad," Mandy said casually. She didn't want her dad to worry about her becoming obsessed with wolves.

"Fine," Dr. Adam replied easily. "Leave the groceries there — I'll put them away."

"Thanks, Dad," said Mandy.

When they reached the village, they followed Cameron's instructions and found the library — a redbrick building with a big window on one side. Inside, the librarian was busy working on the computer.

James tied Blackie's leash to a post near the window, and they pushed open the door and went inside. It was warm and quiet with children's drawings hanging on the bookshelves. In one corner there were tables and chairs where you could sit and read. An elderly white-haired man was dozing over a newspaper.

The librarian was young with long blond hair held back by a headband. She looked up inquiringly. "May I help you?" she asked in a soft voice.

"We're visitors here, so we don't have a library card," Mandy began. "But we wondered if we could look up some information about wolves?" she finished, looking expectantly at the young woman.

"Well, we have something better than that," the librarian said, smiling at them both. "We have the real thing in the wildlife park up the road — beautiful creatures! I took my little girl to see them last week." She bent over and rummaged in a drawer. "Here's a form for you to fill out," she said.

"You don't mind the wolves living nearby?" Mandy asked, glancing at James and raising her eyebrows in surprise. "We heard that there was some opposition."

"Yes, but most of us are in favor of the park. It does very useful work, you know," she said, sitting up straight again. "Here we are. Just fill in your name and address. I'll show you where to look."

After a few minutes the librarian, Mandy, and James had gathered armfuls of books.

"Phew!" said James as they piled them on a table.

"Have fun," said the librarian, before going back to her desk.

Mandy's heart sank. There were at least ten big, thick books. "We'll be here forever!" she told James.

"It won't take long to find what we want," James said encouragingly. "I'm a little worried that Blackie might get cold outside, though."

They glanced out of the window. Blackie was lying down with his head on his paws. As if she read their minds, the librarian came over to them. "It's not strictly allowed, but if you're going to be in here for a while, you may as well bring your dog in. We don't want it stuck frozen to the ground out there, do we?" she said.

James dashed outside before she could change her mind and got Blackie. To their surprise, Blackie lay down beside James at once. He was so quiet that they almost forgot he was there.

"He must know that he'll be sent out into the cold if he's noisy," James said quietly.

Mandy and James leafed through the books but couldn't find anything specific enough about wolves that were native to Scotland. Mandy was just beginning to lose hope when James exclaimed loudly, "Yes! Here it is."

The librarian looked over at them and frowned.

"Sorry," James mouthed back as he pushed the book toward Mandy. "Look," he told her. "Here it is! Everything we need."

Mandy and James shared the book and began to read. Soon they had discovered that most of Scotland was once covered by great ancient forests that were full of wild animals.

"Look at this," James whispered to Mandy. "There used to be bears here, too. The last one was killed a thousand years ago."

"But what about wolves?" Mandy asked. "When was the last wolf seen?" She turned a page and gasped. There were several photographs showing the methods used to kill wolves.

"Yuck!" James declared softly, anger in his voice. "Can you imagine getting caught in that!" he said, pointing to a picture of a large metal trap. Two rows of sharp-looking, pointed teeth surrounded a flat metal plate. "They bury it in the ground," James explained, "and when something steps on the plate, it triggers the jaws to snap shut!"

Mandy shuddered. She couldn't imagine how terrifying it would be to be caught in such a trap. She imagined it clamping shut with a horrible metal clang. She turned the page quickly.

A headline glared out at her — *"The Last Wild Wolf in Scotland."* With a sinking heart, Mandy began to read.

"Oh, no!" she exclaimed, and read aloud, *"The last known wolf in Scotland was shot in 1743."* Mandy carefully closed the book. "There couldn't be any left now, could there, James?" she asked, her voice tiny with defeat.

James shook his head. "Not after all this time. I'm sure someone would have seen them," he said sadly. "I've found some more facts about wolves, though." He opened a book and flicked through until he found what he was looking for. "This book says that wolves are *very* intelligent. Apparently, each wolf's howl is different and wolves can recognize one another's howls from several miles away. They live in family packs, where older wolves look after younger ones and the top wolf — the head of the pack — is called the alpha male. It also says . . ." James paused and looked seriously at Mandy.

"Go on, tell me," Mandy said glumly. She guessed from James's expression that she wasn't going to like what he had to say.

"Well, it says that wolves are often killed because people are frightened of them, not because they've attacked humans," James said, shutting the book. "Wolves seem to be having a pretty rough time every-where. They're endangered in lots of countries."

"All the more reason for them to stay at the wildlife park," Mandy said, her voice rising. "It's time . . ."

"*Shhhh!*" The white-haired man had woken up and was glaring at them.

"It's time," Mandy whispered to James, "that there were a lot more wolves around, *I* think."

"We'll be closing soon," the librarian called over to them.

Mandy looked out of the window. It was beginning to get dark. "We'd better hurry," she said, piling the books on top of one another. "We don't want to get lost."

They thanked the librarian and set off for the estate.

"Imagine, when this was all forest, there would have been bears and wolves *everywhere*," Mandy said, spreading her arms wide.

"And lynx and wild cattle and elk," James added. "I bet it was a really wild place to be."

"It's sort of sad, isn't it?" said Mandy as they walked past the main house and turned down the path. "To think that whole species of animals disappeared from this area before we even had a chance to see the animals in the wild."

"That's why wildlife parks are important," said James.

Dusk was just falling when they emerged from the woods and saw the lights of the lodge. Mandy realized that they'd missed lunch completely. Oatmeal *must* be filling.

Later that evening, after a meal of vegetarian chili and salad, they sat by the fire in the living room. Blackie kept well out of the reach of the sparks.

"I meant to tell you, while I was getting dinner ready, I heard a news item about the young wolves at the wildlife park," Dr. Emily said.

Mandy and James sat up quickly.

"What did it say?" Mandy asked urgently. "I can't believe that I missed it!"

"It's all right, Mandy. I listened very carefully." Dr. Emily gave her a knowing smile. "I knew you'd want to hear all about it. Apparently, the wolves are captive-bred juveniles, less than two years old. They're from different packs — the hope is that eventually they will breed."

"Great," Mandy said.

"That's the good news, Mandy," her mom said. "The bad news is that the local farmers and ranchers are campaigning against them."

"But it's so wrong!" Mandy started to say more, but Dr. Emily shook her head.

"They have a right to their point of view, Mandy," she said. "They do have their livelihoods to worry about. They're worried that the wolves might escape and start killing their livestock."

"But we read up about wolves this afternoon. Hundreds of years ago, before people started killing lots of them, wolves used to keep the deer herds under control naturally," Mandy explained.

"But things were quite different then," Dr. Emily said. Then she softened. "I certainly don't agree with the farmers. They want to get rid of them any way they can."

Mandy was horrified. "What could they do?" she asked urgently.

"I hope they're not talking about using traps," Dr. Adam said from the depths of an armchair. "Those contraptions are positively barbaric. And illegal as well."

Mandy clenched her fists. She could feel anger welling up inside her as she remembered the trap that she'd read about in the library book. She slipped off her shoes, drew her feet up onto the chair, and sat hugging her knees. In the background, she could hear her parents and James talking, but she couldn't stop thinking about the young wolves' predicament.

Suddenly, Mandy began to feel uncomfortable. It was as if someone were watching her. Glancing around the room, her gaze was drawn to the window. Mandy felt her body go rigid and held her breath. It was there! The wolf was there! It was staring right at her.

This time, it couldn't possibly be her imagination. The wolf was enormous — Mandy could see its great mane of white fur shining in the moonlight. And its gaze was so intense that it seemed to bore right into her. She stared back at the wolf, not daring to look away for an instant, in case it disappeared.

"Mandy!" She could hear her mom calling her. Mandy didn't want to move, even to nod her head.

"Dad's suggesting we go to the wildlife park tomorrow," Dr. Emily said, then laughed. "Would you like to go, or is that a silly question?"

Mandy knew she had to respond. For a second, she dragged her gaze away from the sad yellow eyes of the great wolf to nod agreement to her mom.

But when she looked back, the wolf was gone.

Four

"Or would you rather do something else?" Dr. Adam was saying as Mandy refocused on the room. She looked at the expectant faces of her parents and James. They were all waiting for an answer.

"Yes, of course," Mandy said quickly, trying to keep her voice normal and wondering what on earth they'd been saying.

"Which one? You'd like to visit the wildlife park?" Dr. Adam asked, his eyes twinkling. "Or do something else?"

"The wildlife park, please," said Mandy, trying desperately to resist the urge to keep glancing at the window.

"Good, then that's settled," said Dr. Adam, standing up and walking across to the dresser. "Look what I discovered this morning." He opened the cupboard and pointed to an assortment of board games. "Who's up for a game of Scrabble?"

Mandy tried, but she just couldn't concentrate. She was thinking so hard about the old wolf that she almost jumped out of her skin when her mom snapped her fingers in front of her face.

"What's going on in there, Mandy Hope?" asked Dr. Emily, giving her a concerned smile. "You're not with us tonight, are you?"

"Sorry, Mom," Mandy said, shrugging her shoulders. "I can't seem to concentrate."

"It wouldn't have anything to do with wolves at the window?" Dr. Emily asked, sighing and raising her eyebrows. "Don't you think that if there *were* wolves roaming the Mudie Estate, someone would have seen them?"

"I know," Mandy said, nodding slowly. "It's just . . . well, it's nothing really." She didn't want to worry her parents. Now James was giving her a peculiar look, too. "All right, then," she said brightly. "Who's winning?"

But Mandy was too far behind to catch up, so James had a spectacular win.

*   *   *

That night, Mandy lay tossing and turning in bed for what seemed like hours.

Am I ever *going to get to sleep tonight?* she asked herself as she tossed and turned for the hundredth time. She lay and listened to the reassuring sounds of the forest. An owl was hooting to its mate and, in the distance, she heard the sharp bark of a fox. Then, just as she was drifting off to sleep at last, she was startled wide awake.

Clang!

The ominous clanging sound of metal hitting metal seemed very near. Mandy lay motionless in the bed, frantically trying to figure out what it was she'd heard.

Metal hitting metal? Mandy thought, feeling a cold shiver run through her. *A trap! That's what it must have been — a trap snapping shut.* She sat bolt upright in bed and cracked her head on the beam. *They could be out in the forest setting traps right now!* Mandy jumped out of bed and flew to the window. She pushed it open and leaned out as far as she could.

The howl began low and slow. Mandy's scalp prickled and she felt as if her blood had run cold. Gradually, it built up until it was a deafening *"AWOOOOO"* that echoed off the hills. Then, abruptly, the howling stopped. Mandy craned her neck to catch the last echoes as they faded away.

The forest was now silent and still. Mandy was frozen to the spot, her breath steaming in the icy air. There *was* a wolf out there. Surely, everyone must have heard that eerie howling?

Mandy stood in her bedroom trying to calm herself down and wondering what to do next. Her first reaction had been to wake her parents, but something made her hesitate. Why hadn't they — and James — come rushing out to tell *her* about it?

Gradually, she realized how cold she was getting and how tired she was. Maybe now she would be able to sleep. She reached for the icy handle on the window to pull it shut.

Whooosh!

Suddenly, a gust of air rushed past Mandy's ears and something soft touched her hair. She gasped, staggered backward, and then heaved a sigh of relief when she saw an owl swoop away into the darkness. Its silent wings had brushed her head.

Mandy leaned against the window and laughed silently to herself. She really was letting the business with the wolf get to her. She would find out about the clanging noise the next morning, but now she was going back to bed — to sleep!

Suddenly, she heard the scraping sound of her bedroom door opening. Mandy spun around in alarm. "Who is it?" she hissed. "James, is that you?"

But there was no answer and still the door continued to move. Now, Mandy could hear another sound — *thump, thump, thump!* Clenching her fists defiantly, she took a step forward. "Who's there?" she said, yanking the door open with all her strength.

Standing in the doorway, tail thumping against the door frame, was Blackie.

"Blackie!" Mandy cried out with relief. "What are you trying to do? You almost frightened me to death!"

She switched on the light and looked around the room. Everything seemed perfectly normal. "What's the matter with me, Blackie?" She grinned as she bent down to rub his head. "First I get spooked by a toad, then a clanging noise, then a wolf, then an owl — and now a dog!"

Blackie just seemed to grin back at her as he rolled over and thumped his tail on the floor.

Mandy could see light coming from James's room. Blackie must have pushed open the door and sneaked out. She tapped softly on the door and went in to find James deeply engrossed in a computer magazine.

"Blackie just pretended to be a ghost," she told James.

"He does things like that at night." James laughed. "He must've done it to make you jump."

"He did!" she agreed. "Especially coming right after that clanging noise and the howling."

"Howling?" James said in a puzzled voice. "Clanging?" He wrinkled up his nose. "I don't know what you're talking about."

"You were awake," Mandy said, staring at him in amazement. "You *must* have heard it."

"It has been very quiet tonight," James said, closing his magazine. "I did hear an owl and I thought I heard a fox bark, but I'm not sure."

"But there was a clanging noise, like the jaws of a trap closing," Mandy said desperately. "Then I heard a wolf howling — a really sad, lonely howl. It sounded like it was coming from the forest. How did you miss it? It went on for *ages*!"

"Nope! Didn't hear any of that," James said, shaking his head. He looked at his watch. "It is very late. Are you sure it wasn't a dream?"

"Of course it wasn't," Mandy said indignantly. "How could I have dreamed it when I was wide awake? You were more likely to fall asleep reading that boring magazine." She scratched Blackie's head. "I mean, you didn't even notice that Blackie had left your room."

"That's true," James agreed.

But once she was back in bed, Mandy knew that James could not possibly have missed the wolf's howling. She'd heard it. So why hadn't he? She was still puzzling over this when she eventually fell asleep.

Bonnng!

Mandy woke with a start. Not *more* loud clanging noises!

"Breakfast is served," her dad called up the stairs in a snooty voice, trying to sound like an old-fashioned butler. "And if you're not up in five minutes, I'll come upstairs and bang this gong again!"

She looked at her watch. She'd overslept. She felt as if she needed at least two more hours' sleep, but remembered that they were going to the wildlife park today. Suddenly filled with energy and enthusiasm at the thought of seeing the two young wolves, she sprang out of bed, dressed quickly, and ran downstairs.

Her dad was standing in the hall, with the gong ready for action. Mandy put her hands over her ears as Dr. Adam hit it firmly with a leather-covered mallet.

"I've always wanted to do that," Dr. Adam said in a satisfied voice. "These were used to call people to meals in the olden days."

"Was that when you were a boy, Dad?" Mandy asked with a grin, ducking out of the way and dodging into the kitchen. "Where's James?" she asked her mom.

As if in answer to her question, James and Blackie burst in through the back door. Blackie's leash was trailing behind him, and James looked exhausted. "Blackie . . . walk . . ." He panted and flopped into a chair. Within seconds, he was joined by everyone else. Soon they were all enjoying plates of fluffy scrambled eggs and toast, washed down with mugs of tea.

"We can go to the wildlife park right after breakfast," Dr. Emily said, reaching for the teapot. "That will give us lots of time. We could even have lunch there. More toast, James?"

"Thanks," James said, taking a slice. "I can't wait to see the wolves. I wonder how big they'll be."

"A good size, I imagine. They won't be little pups anymore," Dr. Adam said. "Nowhere near as heavy as an adult, though — *they* can weigh up to a hundred pounds."

Mandy looked thoughtful. "I wonder how close we'll be able to get to them," she said.

"We'll soon find out," Dr. Emily said with a smile. "It won't take long to get there. And if we're all finished eating," she said, beginning to clear the table, "we can go."

James looked sternly at Blackie, who had jumped up and made for the door. "I'm afraid you've got to stay here," he told him. "Dogs aren't allowed in the wildlife park. But we'll take you out for a long walk when we get back, I promise."

"I'm going to cook this afternoon," Dr. Adam told them as he started the engine of the Animal Ark Land Rover. "There's a wonderful old cookbook in the dresser drawer. It's got a recipe for neeps and tatties. That's turnips and potatoes to you two."

"Sounds good," James said, latching his seat belt.

Though the wildlife park had been set up on land belonging to the Mudie Estate, the entrance was a few miles away. They drove out of the estate and along narrow winding lanes, following signs for MUDIE WILDLIFE PARK. Dr. Adam turned up the driveway and drove through an ivy-covered stone entrance and past a group of old buildings, before following a sign to the parking lot. When they got out of the Land Rover, a tall man with a shock of white hair came striding toward them.

"Welcome," he called to them, holding out his hand in greeting to Drs. Adam and Emily. "You must be Angus's veterinarian friends. I'm glad to meet you. I'm Duncan Marriott and I run this place." He had deep-blue eyes that crinkled up when he smiled. He was wearing khaki trousers and a thick sweater in deep forest-green. MUDIE WILDLIFE PARK was embroidered neatly in red on the top pocket.

"And you must be Mandy and James," he said, shaking hands with them both. "Angus tells me that you like animals as much as I do. That takes some doing!"

Mandy knew immediately that she was going to like this man.

"How did you know who we were?" Dr. Adam said, looking faintly surprised.

"You advertised yourself," Duncan said, pointing to the Animal Ark logo on the Land Rover's door. "Come and meet my wife, Sally. If you like, we'll take you around the park ourselves!"

"That's very kind of you," Dr. Emily said. "But we don't want to disturb you if you're busy."

"No, no," Duncan said, smiling at them. "I always check the park thoroughly every morning. It'll be nice to have some company."

"We might be able to get really close to the animals," Mandy whispered to James as they followed Duncan into his office.

"Angus's friends have arrived," Duncan said to a woman sitting behind a desk. "Here's Sally. She handles most of the paperwork and keeps this place running," he told them.

Sally stood up and came out from behind the desk. "I'm very pleased to meet you," she said when Dr. Emily had introduced them all. Sally had a soft lilting voice, long blond hair tied back in a ponytail, and a smile as friendly as her husband's.

"I'm taking them around," Duncan told her. "Can you join us?" He turned to the Hopes and James. "As well as the office work, Sally is responsible for the gift shop and supervises the restaurant. She also takes care of any young or sick animals."

"You must be busy!" exclaimed Dr. Adam.

"It keeps me on my toes." Sally laughed. "My favorite job at the moment is rearing our two new arrivals."

Mandy felt a tingle of excitement. "The wolves?" she asked Sally.

"Yes," she replied, smiling. "They are absolutely gorgeous — wait until you see them. And they're *so* intelligent, too."

"It must be hard work, all this," Dr. Emily said, indicating the park with her arm.

"It is," Sally agreed. "But at least we have more help now. Before that, we were cleaning the animals as well! Let's go!" she said, getting her coat. "I have some time to spare — we don't get as many visitors during the winter."

Mandy and James walked beside Sally, while Mandy's parents followed behind Duncan. They all listened avidly as he explained the workings of a wildlife park.

Sally stopped at a large wooden building, took out a bunch of keys, and unlocked the door.

"Once a week, the animals get a treat," she told Mandy and James. "Would you like to come and help me?"

They followed her inside. The walls were lined with shelves stacked with old newspapers, buckets, brooms, and brushes. Shovels and rolls of fencing were propped against the walls. In the corner, there was a wheelbarrow full of loaves of bread and cakes.

"Here we are," Sally said, handing them the wrapped loaves. "Donald at the mini-market lets us have everything from the bakery that hasn't been sold."

Loaded up with loaves and cakes, Mandy and James followed Sally and Duncan to the first enclosure. They stopped in front of a sturdy wooden barrier with a deep ditch on the other side. In the middle of the enclosure was a large rocky area surrounded by woodland. "This is where Dolly lives," Duncan said, leaning on the fence. Mandy looked around the field but couldn't see any animals at all.

"Rustle the bags," Duncan told them.

Mandy and James shook the paper bags that contained the cakes. Within seconds, a big brown bear appeared from among the boulders. She loped over to them and then stood up on her back legs and pawed the air with her arms.

"Mandy and James — meet Dolly," Sally said gently. "Dolly came here from Eastern Europe. Street vendors had been making money using her. They'd been parading her around and tormenting her to make her dance. She's really gentle now, but when we first got her, she'd been so badly treated that she was terrified and lashed out at everyone." Sally took a doughnut from Mandy's bag. "Throw her this," she said, handing it to Mandy.

Mandy threw the cake and Dolly caught it in her

mouth. "Oh, no!" Mandy cried out. "Look, James! She's got a hole through her nose."

"Animals have very sensitive noses, and they'd put a ring through hers to control her," Duncan explained. "She must have been given a treat now and then, because she certainly loves these cakes!"

Dolly looked expectantly at Mandy, but Duncan and Sally were already walking away. "I'm sorry. No more," Mandy told the bear softly as she and James reluctantly followed them.

"There were bears in Scotland many years ago," Duncan said, his voice wistful. "But they were wiped out by hunters. The same thing happened to the wolves."

On the far side of the next field, they could see a herd of animals grazing on straw. Their heads sprang up when they saw the party.

"Reindeer," Sally explained as they trotted over to the fence. She ripped open a loaf of bread and handed slices to Mandy and James for them to throw. "They're from Sweden. Can you guess the name of that big male?"

"Rudolph?" Mandy asked, and laughed when Sally nodded.

"Eventually, our aim is to breed in captivity all species of animals that once lived in Scotland," Duncan said as they moved on again. "Then people can appreciate how much we've lost."

Twenty minutes later they had fed the Shetland ponies and the wild boar, before stopping at an enclosure containing a pair of pine martens.

"Weren't these almost wiped out?" Dr. Adam asked Duncan.

"You're right. They were once on the verge of extinction, mainly because of snares," Duncan answered. "Good conservation work saved them, that and banning traps."

"We heard some people complaining about the wolves yesterday," Mandy said, her face full of concern.

"Some of them were really angry," James added.

Duncan put his hands on his hips and stared into the distance. "I know, but they really don't need to be worried. The wolves can't escape," he said with a pained expression. "They've settled in well. But, like a lot of young animals, they're frisky and full of energy. They're bound to be seen charging around the enclosure, and that can give the public the wrong impression."

"It doesn't necessarily mean that they're trying to get out," Dr. Adam agreed.

"True." Duncan grinned. "Come on, let's introduce you." And he set off toward the farthest end of the park.

"Their enclosure is really big," said Sally as they walked alongside a tall, solid-looking chain-link fence, at least a hundred yards long. "We wanted it to be as similar to the wolves' natural habitat as possible."

"Will you release the wolves when they're older?" James asked. "That's what some people seemed worried about."

Duncan laughed. "I don't think that's even remotely possible at the moment. There's far too much opposition. And it's something that would need very careful thought and planning. It couldn't be undertaken lightly."

"So they're safe in here?" Mandy asked.

"Definitely. All of the enclosures back onto a high perimeter fence," Duncan explained. "It's made up of two layers of chain link with a gap in between. The outer fence has barbed wire on the top to make it even more secure."

"To keep the animals in?" James asked.

"And to keep people out!" said Sally. "There's also a ditch inside the perimeter fence, so that if it snows heavily and piles up, the animals can't climb out."

"You've thought of everything!" Dr. Adam commented. "I'm impressed."

"This inner fence is strong, too," Duncan said, pushing hard at the fence to prove it. "It's buried very deep in the ground, so it's virtually impossible to dig underneath it. And just to keep people happy, we're going to make the fence even higher."

Sally put her hand on Mandy's shoulder. "Look, Mandy," she said in a voice full of excitement. "There they are. What do you think of them?"

Five

Mandy stared through the wire mesh. Bounding toward her were two of the most gorgeous creatures that she had ever seen. The wolves stopped close to the fence and looked at the little party quizzically.

One had a glossy dark-brown coat and a black face with a pink spot on its nose. The other was beige colored with a gold stripe on its nose and gold-tipped ears.

"They look like big German shepherd puppies, but their coats are so thick and long," Mandy said in an awed voice. "Do they let you pet them?" she asked Sally.

Sally nodded. "Right now they think I'm their mom.

They're not big enough yet to be able to fend for themselves completely. Would you like to meet them?"

"Meet them?" Mandy repeated, looking up at her parents.

"You mean — go inside the enclosure?" added James.

Dr. Adam grinned. "We weren't expecting this, were we?" he said as Mandy and James looked back in amazement.

Duncan unlocked the outer gate, and they filed through into a safety cage with a gate at the other side. Sally waited for Duncan to lock the outer gate before unlatching the inner one. "Let me go first to get them settled," she said softly.

The young wolves ran to Sally and rubbed their bodies against her legs. Then she beckoned to Mandy.

Mandy felt excitement tingle through her body as, with Duncan beside her, she walked toward the wolves. They stared at her, eyes wide with curiosity, then trotted over. She bent down slowly and began to stroke their thick coats.

"You *are* wonderful!" she said, running her hand down the dark wolf's back and along its bushy tail. "What big feet you have." Not to be left out, the beige wolf nudged at her knees, trying to push the dark wolf out of the way. One by one, James and her parents came

across — soon they were all making a fuss about the young wolves.

"As they get older, they won't be able to have contact with humans. They'll need their wolf instinct if they are ever going to form a pack."

Dr. Emily looked at her watch. "I think we've kept these kind people from their work long enough. Why don't we have some lunch?" she suggested.

"Can we come later?" Mandy pleaded as they left the enclosure. "I'm not hungry, and there's so much more to see!"

"You're never hungry when there are animals to be seen, Mandy," Dr. Adam said. "But what about you, James?"

"I'm starving!" James burst out. Then, seeing the disappointment on Mandy's face, backtracked. "No, actually, I don't think I'm *really* hungry, not yet," he said, his face turning pink as everyone laughed.

"Why don't you go and see the Soay sheep, Mandy?" Sally suggested after Dr. Emily had nodded her approval. "And the Highland cattle are worth a look, too."

Mandy glanced back at the wolves. They were bouncing around each other like overgrown puppies, chasing each other's tails.

"I wonder if we'll get a chance to come back and see

them again before we go home," Mandy said, going off around the park. "Aren't they gorgeous?"

"I thought they'd look alike," said James, falling into step with Mandy. "I didn't realize there was such variety in the colors and patterns of their coats."

They found the Highland cattle, with their long, shaggy coats and enormous horns. Then they visited the brown-fleeced Soay sheep. The sign said that these were the only really wild sheep in Scotland. They were beautiful but Mandy couldn't tear her thoughts away from the wolves.

"Can you imagine how big and powerful they'll be when they're full grown?" she said to James as they made their way back to the restaurant.

"Wow, you're not kidding," James agreed. "They wouldn't want to play with you then. They'd be too busy hunting."

Mandy and James arrived at the restaurant just as everyone's lunch was served. Luckily for James, Dr. Emily hadn't forgotten them and he eagerly bit into his pizza.

By the time they'd said good-bye to the Marriotts and driven back to the lodge, it was midafternoon.

"Come on, James," Mandy said as she jumped out of the Land Rover. "We promised Blackie that we'd take him for a walk."

"Wait a minute," James called after her. "Look who's coming down the path."

Mandy turned to see Cameron sprinting down the path from the main house with Beattie at his heels.

"Hello," he said, puffing slightly. "I saw you drive in and thought I'd catch you. Would you like to come and see the house and my project this afternoon? You could stay for dinner as well, if you like."

Mandy looked at her parents. "Is that OK, Mom?" she asked.

"Of course! How nice of you to invite them, Cameron," Dr. Emily said. "But they *must* take Blackie out for a long walk first. He's been inside since this morning."

"That's fine with me. Beattie and I will come along, too," Cameron said. He looked down at Beattie, who was wiggling her body and wagging her tail with excitement, and grinned. "But I can't guarantee that she'll keep up with Blackie!"

"We don't mind," Mandy said, bending down and stroking the little chocolate-colored dog. "She's *so* sweet."

James freed Blackie from the house and they went off into the woods. After being shut in for so long, Blackie was full of energy — darting all over the place, sniffing scents, and chasing falling leaves. Beattie ran from one side of the path to the other, trying to keep up with him on her short legs.

"Blackie's given her a new lease of life," Cameron said. "She hasn't been this active in months."

"Mom and Dad sometimes tell people with old dogs that a puppy might help liven them up," Mandy said.

"Maybe you should get Beattie a friend," James suggested.

"Maybe I will," Cameron agreed.

They were busy talking about dogs and puppies and about life at Animal Ark when James stopped suddenly. "Where are we now? I can't hear the dogs."

Cameron stopped and looked around. "We've gone a long way. This is where the estate borders the wildlife park. Beattie!" he called, loud and clear.

They stood still and listened for a sound. Nothing.

"Blackie, here, boy! Come!" James shouted.

Mandy put her hand up to silence him. "I can hear noises over there," she said, pointing over to the right.

As they watched, Blackie came into view among the distant trees. "See," James said proudly. "He's very obedient, really."

Mandy and Cameron looked at each other, and both burst out laughing.

"You wish, James," Mandy said, grinning broadly.

Just when James agreed in a good-natured way, Blackie began barking. Then, suddenly, the sound was cut off by a terrible clanging noise. Mandy recognized it immediately as the same sound that she had heard last night. Metal hitting metal. She felt light-headed and faint and shook her head to clear the sensation.

"What was that?" James and Cameron said together.

But, before Mandy could answer, they heard a dreadful scream and howl of pain. She knew for certain that it wasn't a wolf. It was Blackie.

Mandy saw the blood drain out of James's face as he dashed off toward Blackie.

Mandy raced after James. *Please don't let Blackie be hurt*, she said to herself. *Please!*

She could feel Cameron running close behind her. *He must be just as worried about Beattie*, she thought. They hurtled up and over a small hill and there, huddled and trembling in a ditch, licking his paw, was Blackie. Standing guard beside him, wide-eyed and shivering with fright, was Beattie.

"Blackie!" James cried in a worried voice. Slipping and sliding, he scrambled down into the ditch and buried his face in his dog's neck. Cameron climbed down and scooped up his little dog. Mandy watched James and Blackie, her vision blurred with tears. She half fell into the ditch and quickly helped to examine Blackie's paw.

"James?" she said urgently, nudging his arm. "James, I'm sure it's not too bad."

James lifted an anxious face. "I know, Mandy. It's just that I was so scared," he said in a voice thick with relief. "I couldn't bear it if anything happened to him."

Blackie had had enough of being hugged to death and was struggling to get up. But every time he tried, he yelped in pain.

"Look, James," Mandy said, gently running her hand down the dog's foreleg. "See, his leg's bleeding." Blackie gave a soft yelp and looked at Mandy with reproachful eyes. "Don't worry, Blackie," she said. "We'll carry you back to the lodge."

"He's had a close shave, you know," Cameron said, his voice somber. "Look here."

There, hidden in the grass and staked to the ground, was a metal trap. Its vicious teeth were clenched together.

"Blackie could have lost a leg in that, or worse!" Cameron said angrily. "Ranchers once used them. It's virtually impossible for a creature to escape," he said, nodding. "Animals have been known to chew their own legs off to try to get free."

Mandy shuddered. "We need to get Blackie back to

Mom and Dad so they can treat him," she said, beginning to get angry at whoever had set the trap. They must have known what injuries they could cause.

"I'll wait here," Cameron said, sitting down with Beattie on his lap. "Could you call the police and tell Officer Farish what happened? These traps are illegal. My dad will need to know about it, too, since it was set on his land."

James took off his coat and made a sling for them to carry Blackie home.

"Be careful where you walk, now," Cameron warned them. "Whoever set that trap could have set others."

As they carried Blackie home, Mandy began to realize something.

"James, do you remember that noise I heard last night?" she said urgently. "Don't you see what this means? It *was* real after all. I didn't dream it or imagine it. Someone *was* out there setting traps, and I *heard* them!"

James paused for a second and glanced up from watching where he was treading. "What about the howl? They didn't catch a wolf, did they?" he said cautiously.

"There *is* a wolf, James." Mandy's voice was positive. "I can't prove it yet, but I will."

They emerged from the trees in front of the lodge,

where they could see Mandy's dad getting something out of the Land Rover.

"Dad!" Mandy shouted at the top of her voice. She could see him looking frantically around. "Over here," she yelled.

Dr. Adam ran up to them. "What's wrong? What's happened to Blackie? Here, give him to me," Dr. Adam said briskly. He carefully took the coat with Blackie inside from James. Mandy ran alongside, explaining all about the traps.

"And will you phone Officer Farish and Cameron's dad, please?" she asked her dad as they arrived at the lodge. Dr. Emily had come out to see what was happening and met the party at the door.

"You deal with Blackie, Emily. I'll go and phone Angus," Dr. Adam said, putting James's dog down carefully on the rug in the kitchen.

"Could you run into our bedroom for me, Mandy?" asked Dr. Emily, but Mandy was already on her way. She ran back into the kitchen with the big black leather bag. Her dad was on the phone in the hall.

"Apparently, Angus. No, Cameron is fine — he's waiting by the trap. Will you call the police?" He hesitated and listened. "Fine, then Mandy can lead us back to him. We'll wait for you here."

"Fortunately, the wound is superficial. But his paw is

badly bruised and sprained," Dr. Emily was saying. "I'll strap it up so that it's not so painful, but he'll need to keep off it for a while. He's got an injury of the carpal joint," she told her husband. "He must've just nicked his leg in the trap and sprained it as he fell."

"From the sound of things, Blackie was lucky," Dr. Adam said, rocking backward and forward on his heels. "What sort of a person sets a steel trap in a private woodland where animals and children run around? It's completely beyond me!"

He walked over to the window and looked out while Mandy helped Dr. Emily strap up Blackie's paw. "Here's the police car now. Angus is in it, too," Dr. Adam said. "James, why don't you stay with Blackie? I'll go with Mandy to find Cameron."

"Thanks," James said gratefully. "I would like to stay with him to help keep him calm."

"He'd better sleep down here tonight," Dr. Emily said, getting up from the floor. "I'll go and get his bed from upstairs."

Mandy and her dad went outside to meet Angus and the police officer.

Angus introduced them and Officer Farish shook hands with them both. He was tall and thin with very short blond hair. In one hand he held a large brown leather bag.

"This is a very bad situation," said the police officer. "I have four dogs of my own at home. The thought of one of them being caught in a trap . . ." he said, smacking his fist into the palm of his other hand. "Lead the way to where you left Cameron, young lady. The sooner we reach him the better," he said, glancing at Angus and Adam.

Mandy guessed that they were worried that the person who set the trap might come back to finish off any poor animal unlucky enough to be caught. Mandy hurried through the woods as fast as she could.

Cameron was sitting with his back against a tree with Beattie asleep in his arms. Dr. Adam gently took the little dog, and Angus helped his son get up.

"Ugh, I'm stiff. I didn't want to move for fear of waking her," Cameron said, stretching his arms above his head. "She's too old to have a shock like this."

Officer Farish was on his hands and knees beside the trap, freeing the stakes out of the ground with a claw hammer. Mandy bent down to look. It sent a shiver through her.

"It's horrible!" the police officer growled, without looking up. "They hammer these so deep into the ground because they know that an injured animal will have the strength of desperation. They can't risk the animal pulling the trap out of the ground and walking off with it attached to its limb."

"What I can't understand is, what are they after?" Angus asked the policeman. "There are no deer in this part of the estate, and I can't believe that anyone around here would go to such trouble for a few rabbits. It's a mystery to me."

Officer Farish had the trap free now, and he zipped it firmly into the leather bag. "I'll make sure that there's a photo of this in the local paper, warning people to watch out," he said. "And I suggest that you be very careful when you're out with the dogs until we've caught whoever is responsible."

The light was fading when they got back to the lodge. It had been a hectic afternoon and they'd all had a fright. Mandy wasn't sorry when Cameron suggested that they visit his house the following morning instead of that evening. But, after supper, she couldn't settle down.

Noticing her restlessness, Dr. Adam said, "If you want a job, Mandy, you can fill the log basket. We're down to our last one." He dropped a log onto the fire.

"OK," said Mandy, springing up and grabbing the basket.

"I'll help you," James said quickly.

In the hall, they grabbed their coats, opened the front door, and stepped outside.

"What do you think is going on in the woods?" James asked, looking at her seriously.

Mandy began loading the basket. "I don't know," she replied.

"But you must have *some* ideas," James persisted. "I know when you've got something on your mind, and tonight you *definitely* have. I'm sure your mom and dad have noticed it, too."

Mandy glanced up at James and said slowly, "I've been thinking about it a lot and I can't come up with anything concrete, but . . ." She paused and stood up, frowning and staring at the trees.

"But?" James prompted.

Mandy turned and looked him in the eye. "I know you don't believe me, but something tells me that it's all about the young wolves — the old wolf, the noises I'm hearing, the trap, everything. It doesn't make much sense, but it's what I believe."

"Mandy, look!" James grabbed her arm. "There's something moving in the woods."

"Where?" She strained to see.

James pointed up the path. "There! In that patch of moonlight, beside that big oak tree! See, it's creeping away."

Mandy made an instant decision. "I'm going to follow it," she said, zipping up her coat. "It could be someone laying more traps. Get Dad!"

"Mandy!" James yelled in protest.

But she was off as fast as her feet would carry her. At the oak tree, she left the path and followed the shape into the woods. She could just make out movement ahead, but it wasn't very clear. She'd have to get closer. A cloud drifted slowly across the bright face of the moon and the forest became so dark that she could hardly see a thing. *I wish I'd brought a flashlight*, she thought.

There was something moving up ahead, silhouetted against the sky. Whatever it was moved deeper and deeper into the forest. She knew that she had no choice — she must follow it or lose it. She sent out a silent message: *Hurry, Dad. Please!*

Suddenly, Officer Farish's words came back to her. *"Be very careful . . ."*

Mandy's heart was in her mouth as she continued walking forward. Before she took each step, she paused with bated breath, for fear of stepping into a trap. The moon came out again and, shocked, she saw that the dark shape was motionless, almost directly ahead of her. Mandy couldn't make out what it was. She stood very still and waited for it to move.

To her horror, it turned and began to walk toward her. And then, with a sick feeling in her stomach, Mandy realized it had been a trick. She had been lured deep into the forest — now the thing was coming back to her.

As the creature drew closer, Mandy could make out a shimmering haze all around. Her eyes widened and she gasped in recognition. It was a wolf. A huge gray wolf.

Mandy half turned and tried to run, but her legs felt as heavy as lead and she couldn't move them. Now she could clearly see a dark T-shaped stripe on the animal's face. It was the wolf she had seen at the window. It padded closer silently.

Then, when it was near enough to touch, it stopped. Its sad yellow eyes bored into hers.

Mandy tried desperately to speak, but she couldn't make a sound.

Six

The old wolf stared at Mandy with its amazingly yellow eyes. It was enormous, with great, powerful jaws, but Mandy didn't feel afraid. She stared back.

In the distance she heard a cry. "Mandy!" It was her dad's anxious voice. "Mandy, where are you?"

Then she heard James's voice, getting closer. "Mandy, can you hear me?"

Without moving its head, the wolf shifted its gaze to a point behind Mandy. It gave her one last piercing look before turning and padding away. Then the wolf melted into the darkness among the trees — and was gone.

Mandy felt drained, as if her body were about to

crumple and collapse. She turned and saw James standing among the trees behind her, staring wide-eyed with amazement.

"You saw it, James, didn't you?" Mandy said urgently. She could hear her dad calling again.

James nodded. "I didn't believe you," he said earnestly. "But I saw it standing there, as large as life."

"Don't say anything yet," Mandy warned as Dr. Adam came running up. "Not till we know what it's all about."

"Are you all right, Mandy?" Dr. Adam gasped as he reached her. Even in the gloom, Mandy could see that his face was very pale and his eyes were dark with worry. "What on earth were you thinking?" he asked, putting his hands on her shoulders. "You had us really worried. Mom was ready to call the police."

"I thought it was the person who set the traps, Dad," she said apologetically. "Once I got into the forest I couldn't see anything. I'm sorry."

Dr. Adam was silent as they left the woods, but once they arrived back at the lodge, he looked at them both intently.

"Now, look here," he said, his voice serious. "We've already had one potentially bad accident today." He glanced up as Dr. Emily came out into the hall. "Your mom will agree. James gave us a terrible shock when he said you were following somebody into the woods.

People who set traps like that are *not* playing games. You might have found yourself in all sorts of trouble."

"But, Dad —" Mandy began.

"No, Mandy, no arguments. I want you both to promise that you will stay out of the woods," Dr. Adam demanded, looking from one to the other. "I mean it. Leave crime solving to the professionals. Let Officer Farish sort it out."

Mandy looked at her parents' faces. She could tell that they were upset, and she felt guilty that she was the cause.

"This is supposed to be a relaxing vacation, Mandy," her mom added reproachfully. "We don't want to have to worry about you two every time you leave the lodge."

"OK," said Mandy glumly. "I'm sorry. I know I shouldn't have run off like that."

"And me," said James. "I'm sorry I scared you, too."

"Then we won't talk about it anymore," Dr. Emily told them. "There's just one more thing, though," she added.

Mandy looked up at her mom with a worried expression. "What is it?"

"The logs . . ." her mom pointed out, smiling broadly.

"Oh, I'd forgotten all about them," Mandy said, heading for the door with James hot on her heels.

"What now?" James asked as soon as they were outside. "What do we do now?"

Mandy's face was set in a frown. "We wait and see what happens next." She sighed. For the second time that evening, she heaved logs into the basket.

"But we can't go in the woods," James said uneasily. "We promised."

"I know, and we may not have to," she said, looking him in the eye. "Don't forget, the wolf has come to the window twice already."

Together, they carried the log-filled basket back inside and both sat where they had a clear view of the windows. But by bedtime, they hadn't seen a thing.

Mandy woke early the next morning. It was still dark, but she could hear James moving around in his room. His door opened and she heard him run downstairs. She smiled to herself. He was anxious to check on Blackie. Soon the tempting smell of bread toasting drifted up the stairs, and Mandy guessed that her dad was up. She dressed and went downstairs.

"Morning, honey," Dr. Adam greeted her. "One round of toast coming shortly."

"Morning, Dad," she replied. "Where's James?"

"Blackie's foot is much better this morning," Dr. Adam told her, smiling. "James has taken him out for a short, gentle stroll."

"Blackie!" Mandy exclaimed. "Strolling gently? That'll be the day."

"I'm afraid that we all — even strong-willed dogs like Blackie — have to bow down to circumstances sometimes!" Dr. Adam said pointedly, giving her a meaningful look.

"It's OK, Dad," Mandy agreed cheerfully. "I promise we'll be good."

"I know you will, honey." Dr. Adam grinned. "Don't frighten us like that again, though. I ran so fast, I could have made the Olympic team."

James came in the kitchen door. "Look, Mandy," he said. "Blackie can almost walk properly."

"Don't let him overdo it, James," Dr. Adam said. "He ought to rest it as much as he can."

"He'd better stay here while we go to Cameron's house, then," Mandy suggested, helping herself to orange juice.

Dr. Adam picked up a tray laden with tea and toast. "As a special treat, Mom's having breakfast in bed today," he said as he carried it out of the room. "She's resting before the party!"

After breakfast, they grabbed their coats and set off for the big house. At the top of the steps in front of the great oak door, Mandy reached for the huge brass door knocker.

"James!" she gasped, recoiling in shock. "Look!"

"Oh, wow!" James said, following Mandy's gaze. "That's impressive." The door knocker was molded into the shape of a wolf's head, with yellow stones for eyes.

"But why?" Mandy was puzzled. "Why a wolf's head?"

"Maybe Cameron can tell us." James shrugged, lifting the knocker and rapping on the door.

Cameron came to the door. "Hello, come in! How's Blackie this morning?" he greeted them anxiously.

"He's much better," James told him, "but Dr. Adam says he's still got to rest."

"Phew!" said Cameron. "I was really worried about him. Beattie was so frightened that she wouldn't go outside the house last night. But she's perked up today, which is a relief."

Mandy looked around. They were standing in a tall hall, in front of a huge pair of wooden doors. These were covered with intricate carvings of animals. On one side of the doors, a winding staircase led up into darkness.

Cameron flung open the doors and took them inside.

"This is the Great Hall," he told them. "The party will be held here tonight."

Mandy and James stared around the vast room. Logs were burning in the grate of a huge stone fireplace. A colorful coat of arms hung above it. A big basket of pinecones stood nearby. "We'll put them on the fire later on — they smell really nice," Cameron added.

Down the center of the room, long tables were covered with white cloths. "The caterers will be here after lunch to prepare the food," Cameron told them as they walked through the room toward a wide staircase at the end. "My parents have gone to the station to pick up some friends from London," he said.

"What a wonderful house to live in!" exclaimed Mandy.

"Well, we only live in a small part of it," said Cameron. "It would cost too much to heat the whole building all of the time."

"What's upstairs?" James asked, looking up the staircase.

"Come and see," replied Cameron, taking the stairs two at a time.

Soon they were looking down on the Great Hall from high above. "This," he said, holding his arms wide apart, "is the Minstrels' Gallery. This is where musicians used to play years ago. Tonight, we'll have a live band up here."

"Wow, it's going to be fantastic." James sighed, walking along the gallery. "What are all these rooms for?" he added.

"We usually keep this area closed off for guests," Cameron explained. "But tonight it'll be full of family and friends."

"How many people are you expecting?" asked Mandy.

"We don't know for sure," Cameron answered her, raising his eyebrows and grinning. "My dad really loves a party, so Mom always asks lots of people from the village. We never know who's going to turn up!"

He led them back downstairs and opened the door into the Mudies' living quarters. "We live in the rooms at the back of the house — they're easier to warm," he said, bending down to scoop up an excited Beattie. "I'm glad Blackie's foot is going to be all right."

"So am I," James agreed, making a fuss over the little dog.

Mandy stroked Beattie's head and looked around. These smaller rooms looked much cozier than some other parts of the house. One wall of the living room was almost covered by photos and another was lined from floor to ceiling with books.

"Some of these books look really old," James said, and Mandy could tell that he was itching to look at them.

"Help yourself," Cameron offered, putting Beattie on the floor. "Just be a little careful with some of the older ones." Soon, James was poring over the books while Mandy studied the photos on the wall.

"These are some of my ancestors," Cameron said proudly. "Mudies have lived in the house for more than three hundred years." He came over and stood next to Mandy. "If you like animals, you'll love the sketchbook."

"What sketchbook?" she asked.

Cameron grinned mysteriously. "It's a very, very old sketchbook — a family heirloom. I'll show it to you." He got a stool, climbed up, and stretched up to the top shelf, scrambling down seconds later with a silver cardboard box.

"Here." He passed the box to Mandy. "Have a look, but please be very careful. It's really old and very fragile."

She put the box on the table and removed the lid. Inside, wrapped in black tissue paper, was a loose-leaf book with a dark green cover. The pages were bound together with thin green ribbon. The book certainly looked very old. Mandy carefully lifted it out and turned to the first page, which was all mottled and yellow with age. But there in the middle of the ancient paper, was a line drawing of a robin. "It's beautiful," she breathed. "James, come and look."

James put down his book and came over to the table. "It's good, isn't it?" he agreed. "It must have been drawn with pen and ink."

Cameron nodded. "We think that they might have been painted with watercolors, but all the colors have faded away over the years," he said.

Mandy turned the page. A portrait of a fox stared out at them.

The next few pictures were of badgers, hedgehogs, and owls. But the next picture was much more elaborate than the rest — it was of a young girl sitting in a glade, surrounded by animals. What caught Mandy's eye was a large dog, curled up at her feet, partly hidden by her long dress.

"Is that her dog?" Mandy called to Cameron, who was in the kitchen making drinks.

"There aren't any dogs in the sketchbook," he answered. "They're all *wild* animals. That's what made Fiona so special."

"What do you mean?" Mandy asked, full of curiosity.

Cameron came back into the room with mugs of hot chocolate and a plate of cookies. "Fiona had a way with wild animals. They used to gather around her every time she went into the woods. She used to play with them as if they were pets."

Mandy looked more closely at the drawing and saw

that birds were perched on the girl's hand and a squirrel nestled on her shoulder.

"But what about this dog?" Mandy persisted, pointing at the picture.

"That's not a dog." Cameron laughed. "That's a wolf!"

Mandy looked across at James, startled. Then, as she gazed at the creature's face, she suddenly felt her head swim. When she looked up again, Cameron and James were staring at her with worried looks.

"Are you OK?" James asked, his face full of concern.

Mandy nodded. "It's just that . . . well, the markings on its face remind me of a wolf that I've seen before," she said cautiously. She wasn't sure what Cameron would think if she told him about her wolf.

James immediately understood. "It's a mark like a T, isn't it?"

"There's a story behind this wolf," Cameron began enthusiastically. "One winter, Fiona was staying here, getting over an illness. Because she hadn't been out for so long, some of the wild animals came close to the house, to see what was wrong. Fiona saw them and went out to join them. But" — he paused to look at their rapt faces — "she wandered much farther than she should have and became weak."

Mandy looked at the drawing more closely. The girl certainly looked frail and delicate. "Go on," she urged Cameron. "What happened?"

"Well, when someone realized that she was missing, a search party was formed and they went out to find her. In those days, people were frightened of wild animals, and the hunters in the party carried guns. . . ." He paused again and looked from Mandy to James.

Mandy frowned. She had a horrible feeling that she wasn't going to like the next part of this story.

"Eventually, they spotted her. She was fast asleep, leaning against a log. But when they got nearer, they saw that it wasn't a log. A huge old wolf was lying right beside her, almost covering her. It sprang up when it saw them coming and started to walk away from them." Cameron stopped speaking.

"And?" Mandy pleaded softly.

"Because wolves were considered a menace, the hunters shot the old wolf dead," Cameron said, his voice cracking slightly. "But, when they reached Fiona, she was warm and dry, even though it was snowing heavily. They realized then that the old wolf had been protecting her. It had been keeping her warm with its body and tail. Some of the men felt very guilty about what had happened."

"They should have!" Mandy said fiercely. "What a *terrible* thing to do. It sounds as if the wolf knew that Fiona would be safe and was leaving to let the search party look after her."

"Were there any other wolves around?" James asked very quietly.

"That's another thing, James," Cameron said with a grimace. "Wolves were never seen again on the Mudie Estate after that. There was talk that Fiona's wolf could even have been the last wolf in Scotland."

"What happened to Fiona?" Mandy asked.

"She was distraught," Cameron said. "She was in such a state that they thought she would become ill again. That's when they gave her the sketchbook, where she drew a beautiful portrait of the wolf. But, it's said that she was so upset about the wolf's death, her tears dropped on the page and the ink ran. To try and cheer her up, they had the door knocker copied from her sketch. Did you notice it on the front door?"

"We certainly did!" Mandy said. "It gave me a shock."

"Why?" Cameron said, looking surprised.

"Um . . . well . . ." Mandy stuttered, swallowing hard. "I just wasn't expecting it, that's all."

"Oh, I see," Cameron said politely, giving her a strange look. "Let me show you the portrait of the wolf, then." He turned to the next page. "That's funny," he exclaimed, looking baffled. "It should be the next picture." Frowning, Cameron turned the pages back and forth. "There's just a blank page here."

"What are those marks?" Mandy stared hard at the blank page. "Look, there are gray splotches on the page."

"I don't really know," Cameron admitted. "I've never noticed this page before. It's much thinner than the other pages, too."

"It's almost transparent, like glass," Mandy observed.

"That's very odd. . . ." Cameron frowned, looking through the pictures a second time. "I'll put it away and ask my parents about it later. Maybe they've taken the page out for some reason." He wrapped the book in the black tissue. "This prevents the light getting in and fading the pictures," he said, climbing back onto the stool and replacing the box.

An hour later, they were in Cameron's bedroom looking at his school project, when they heard a *toot-toot-toot* from outside.

"I promised I'd give Mom a hand with the bags," Cameron said, quickly getting up.

"We'll help, too," Mandy offered. They followed him out the back door, where Cameron's mom was unloading suitcases and bags from the car.

"You must be Mandy and James," Mrs. Mudie said, brushing her dark brown hair back with a gloved hand. "We're so pleased you could all come. It's going to be a great party. Dad's taken our guests up to see the deer," she told Cameron as they picked up the suitcases.

When all the bags had been taken up to the Minstrels' Gallery, Mandy and James decided that it was time for them to go. Cameron saw them to the door.

"Cameron, tell me one more thing," Mandy asked him. "What happened to Fiona?"

He took a very deep breath. "She married my great-great-great-great-great-great-great-great-grandfather," he said, "so her blood is in the Mudie clan."

"How many greats was that?" James said with a gulp.

"Eight," Cameron said, laughing. "But so far, no one in the family has inherited her way with wild animals!"

"Your dad's a vet, though," Mandy pointed out.

"It's not quite the same thing," Cameron said. "Dad says that Fiona's gift was very rare and special. See you tonight," he said, then gave a wicked grin. "You might not recognize me!"

Seven

"I can't believe that Fiona's wolf and our wolf look *so* much alike!" Mandy burst out as soon as the door had closed behind them.

"*And* the door knocker!" James exclaimed, stopping in his tracks. "Its eyes seem to follow you wherever you go."

Mandy turned to look at him. "I know," she said, sighing deeply. "There's something very spooky going on, but I don't have a clue what it is."

"Do you think there *is* a connection between the wolves?" James said uneasily. He ran his hand through his hair and stared hard at Mandy. "But how *can* there be a connection?" he asked, shaking his head. "The wolf in the picture is dead, isn't it? And ours is alive — we've seen it!"

"I just don't know," Mandy answered. "All the time we were looking at Cameron's project, I couldn't stop wondering about all the strange things that keep happening," she added, absentmindedly tapping the heel of her boot on a frozen puddle. "I know that our wolf wants something. I can see it in its eyes."

"Maybe we ought to tell your mom and dad," James suggested.

"I thought about that, but they'd just worry," Mandy said, setting off down the track again.

"Suppose we *never* find out what it's all about?" James exclaimed suddenly.

"It's happening for a reason," Mandy said confidently. "I'm sure of that."

When they arrived at the lodge, the winter sun had almost disappeared, and Dr. Adam was setting the table.

"We're having a really late lunch because there will be lots of food at the party," he said cheerfully. "I've made a big omelette, Spanish style with potatoes. It'll be delicious."

"You're mixing up your countries, Dad." Mandy laughed.

After their meal, Mandy and James cleaned up while Dr. Emily went to unpack their clothes for the big night.

"James, you'd better take Blackie out for some air. He's improving by leaps and bounds," Dr. Adam said. "But he's going to be shut in again this evening."

"Hi, Mom," Mandy said, going into the bedroom and flopping on the bed.

"There, that's the last thing to be ironed," Dr. Emily said to her daughter as she put James's shirt on a hanger. "Would you mind taking it upstairs for me, please? And here's your new pants and top. We'll have to start getting ready soon — I can't wait!"

"I'm looking forward to it, too," Mandy said, excited. But in the back of her mind, she couldn't stop thinking about the wolf she had seen. She took the hangers from her mom and carried them carefully upstairs, hanging James's shirt on the back of his door.

Then she went into her room. *Brrrrrr!* She couldn't believe how icy it was. Quickly hanging up her clothes, Mandy stooped to feel the radiator. It was hot! But she was so cold that she was shivering.

Mandy shook herself. She was letting the wolf get to her so much that she was starting to imagine things. Obviously, she hadn't shut the window properly. She was just crossing the room to check it, when the lights began to flicker. Quickly, she looked around for the candle, but at once the room was plunged into inky blackness. Moonlight flickered through the window. The eerie silver light seemed to dance on the walls and the carpet.

Mandy knew that she should go downstairs and get a flashlight, but she couldn't move. She heard James stomping up the stairs to his room. She desperately wanted to call out to him, but she couldn't speak. She felt as if icy cold fingers were creeping down her spine.

What is happening to me? Mandy thought desperately. And then, from just outside the window came a noise. *Clang!* She felt her heart leap with fear. It was a trap clamping shut!

Turning her head, she stared out of the window — and could hardly believe her eyes.

On the other side of the path, not twenty yards from the lodge and as clear as day in the sharp moonlight, was a wolf. Stealthily and cautiously, it walked out from among the trees and loped down toward the loch. It was followed by another. Then more and more wolves appeared, until a whole wolf pack was streaming out of the forest. The powerful muscles beneath their glossy coats rippled in the moonlight. They stopped to drink at the loch.

Mandy stood mesmerized.

Then, out of the corner of her eye, she spotted movement in the forest. Her heart skipped a beat, then thudded hard. Suppose it was the poachers who'd seen the wolves? What if they were setting *more* traps? Then, out of the dark woods padded a splendid creature, bigger than any other in the pack.

"The old wolf!" Mandy gasped. The animal met her gaze and, as she watched, the others gathered behind it. So, the old wolf with the yellow eyes was the alpha male, the head of the pack.

Suddenly, the lights in the room came back on, and in a flash the eerie scene vanished. Mandy pressed her

nose against the window to peer out, but the landscape was bleak and empty. Not a wolf in sight.

"James!" At once, Mandy ran out and tapped urgently on his door. She was filled with a strange combination of both fear and excitement.

"What's happened?" James said as he opened the door and saw her face shining with excitement.

"Quick, come with me," Mandy hissed. She ran downstairs, opened the front door quietly, and ran swiftly toward the loch.

"Wait for me," James said as he caught up with her. "What's up?"

"When I went into my room just now, it was freezing cold," Mandy hurriedly explained. "Then, when the lights went out, I saw the old wolf." Catching her breath, her voice trailed off when she saw the look on James's face. "He had a wolf pack with him — and they stood here . . ." she finished lamely.

"But they didn't go out," James said, puzzled. "The lights, I mean. They were on all the time." He frowned and looked down at the ground. "And there are no footprints or anything," he said quietly.

"Well, the lights went out in *my* room, and I saw the wolves!" Mandy said in a furious voice. "*What* is going on?"

"Maybe we *should* tell your parents," James said quietly.

Mandy nodded, pushing her hands deep into her pockets. "I would, normally," she said. "But what would I tell them? They think that I imagined the wolf. How can I tell them that I've now seen a whole pack?"

"That's true," James agreed. "We don't have anything concrete to show them."

When they got back, Mandy's mom and dad were getting ready for the party, so Mandy and James went upstairs to get changed, too. Putting on her new turquoise pants and top, Mandy decided to put all thought of wolves out of her mind until the next morning.

"Aren't we spiffy?" Dr. Adam said with a lopsided grin. Both he and James wore crisp white shirts and dark pants. Dr. Emily looked very pretty in a vivid green silk dress.

"Bye, Blackie," Mandy said, scratching the Labrador behind his ears when James came in from the kitchen.

"A special treat," James told him, putting a plate of dog biscuits beside Blackie's bed.

They got their coats, locked the door, and set off for the main house.

As they turned into the driveway, they could hear the faint sound of music. Mandy looked at James and grinned. She felt better already. Two people were greeting guests at the door, but Mandy didn't know either of them. They both wore tweed jackets, tartan kilts, white knee-high socks, and black leather shoes that laced around their ankles. It wasn't until they walked closer that Mandy suddenly realized the doormen were Angus and Cameron.

"You were right," she said, her eyes shining with amusement. "I *didn't* recognize you at all. You look *so* different in a kilt."

"At least you didn't call it a skirt!" Cameron said. "Some people do. This is the Mudie tartan," he told them proudly.

"Welcome, welcome!" Angus Mudie boomed. He invited them inside and closed the door. "You're about the last, I think."

Angus put his arms around Mandy's parents' shoulders and led them into the Great Hall. The tables were laden with plates and bowls of delicious food. Meanwhile, up in the gallery, a band provided background music.

"Help yourselves to whatever you want," Angus said to Mandy and James. "I'll take your parents to get a drink first."

They joined the line of people and had soon piled

their plates high. Then they found somewhere to sit and eat.

"Look," Mandy said, nudging James. "See that man in the green kilt by the stairs?" She waited till James saw him.

"It's the man who was in the store complaining about the wolves," James said softly, finishing the last chunk of garlic bread on his plate.

Mandy nodded. "Brett McCatter. And there's Donald from the mini-market," she said, nodding toward the window. He was standing with a woman wearing a long skirt in a tartan that matched his kilt. Donald saw Mandy looking over and waved. She waved back at once, smiling.

When everybody had finished eating, waiters collected the plates and cleared the tables. Then there was a drumroll from up in the balcony and one of the musicians stood up.

"Quiet, please, for the piper," he announced in a booming voice.

Within seconds, everyone was waiting expectantly. The door behind them opened and the ghostly wail of bagpipes playing "Happy Birthday" rang out. Then a piper in full regalia appeared, followed by two men carrying an enormous birthday cake decorated with blazing candles. They all joined in singing, and Mandy could hear her dad's strong voice above all the others. Angus blew out the candles and everybody cheered. When Mrs. Mudie began cutting the cake, Cameron came over.

"Could you two help me hand the cake out?" he asked.

"I can hardly move," Mandy joked. "I've eaten too much."

"Me, too," James added.

"Then the exercise will do you good!" Cameron laughed. "Come with me."

At the table, they got trays covered with pieces of cake wrapped in napkins and offered them to all of the guests. They had just finished when the musician announced that there would be dancing in a few moments. Everyone immediately formed themselves into groups and waited for the music to start.

"Let's go, James," Dr. Emily said, grabbing his arm. "You can be my partner."

James blushed, but followed Dr. Emily. Dr. Adam offered Mandy his arm and they, too, found a space on the crowded dance floor. Soon they were laughing fit to burst when they tried to copy the steps and follow the rest of the dancers. It seemed as if they'd only just begun when the last dance of the night was announced.

"But I was just getting the hang of it!" protested Dr. Adam, gasping with laughter.

"I don't think I've got the energy for this," Dr. Emily admitted. "It's been wonderful, but I'm exhausted."

"You have to dance the last one," Dr. Adam said, linking his arm in hers. "I'll hold you up. It's bound to be a slow one!"

But the music got faster and faster and soon everybody was dancing wildly, spinning around in the hall. Mandy lost sight of her mom and dad and just managed to hang on to James's arm. When the dance ended, they all clapped and cheered. The band continued to play popular Scottish tunes as Mandy sank in a chair to get her breath back. Lots of people still seemed to have some energy left and stood around the room, chatting to one another.

"Phew, I'm tired," Cameron said as he joined them. "Did you enjoy the dancing?" He looked hot and flung his jacket on a chair as he sat down.

"It was a lot of fun," Mandy answered. "But pretty energetic." She almost had to shout to be heard over the noise in the room. "Why didn't Sally and Duncan come?"

"They had to go to Edinburgh today for an important conference on wildlife parks," Cameron said. "It's been arranged for a long time. They said that they'll call in on their way home if they have time." He frowned suddenly.

"What's the matter?" Mandy asked.

Cameron stood up. "I thought I heard someone knocking," he said, crossing to the door.

Mandy and James heard it, too. *Bang, bang, bang.*

Cameron looked around the door. "What's up, Gary?" he asked, opening the door to reveal a young man wearing dirty blue overalls and muddy boots. His red hair was lank and greasy, and he had a furious expression on his face. Pushing past Cameron, he strode in to the Great Hall. Everyone fell silent as he appeared.

"There's trouble in the wildlife park!" he shouted so that everyone could hear. "The wolves have gotten out," he explained, looking at the astonished faces around him.

"I'm sure there's nothing to worry about," said Donald's wife. "Duncan and Sally will soon have them back in the enclosure."

Several people in the crowd nodded agreement and began to move around again, murmuring to one another, but Gary had more to say.

"No! You don't understand!" he yelled, and every head turned to him again. "The wolves have escaped from the *wildlife park* — they're running wild in the woods. None of the livestock is safe."

A hush fell on the room broken only by one man's voice.

"I knew it!" he thundered. The crowd parted, and a man came striding toward the door. He thumped his fist on the nearest table, making glasses and bottles rattle together. "I *said* this would happen — and I've been proven right!"

In a flash, Mandy was on her feet with James, craning to see the angry man. Her spirits sank when she saw that it was Brett McCatter.

"They've got to be stopped, and stopped for good!" he went on ominously, looking around the room. "We can't take a chance that this won't happen again. Who's coming with me?"

"I am," a voice came from the back. Mandy recognized the man from the store who owned a herd of deer.

"And us!" Two men standing nearby stepped forward.

"Me, too," Gary added.

"Let's go, then," McCatter said. "I've got my guns in the van."

Mandy desperately looked around for her parents. Normally, her dad would try to defuse such a situation. But the Hopes were nowhere in sight.

"My dad will have something to say about this," Cameron said boldly, standing in front of McCatter. "After all, it's his wildlife park."

"But the wolves are not *in* the park anymore," Mc-Catter spat out, waving him aside. "That's the trouble."

Everybody surged forward.

"We've got to stop them," Mandy said urgently to James and Cameron, who were staring in horror at the group of men hurrying out of the door. They all knew what would happen to the young wolves when they were found. "James, can you look for Cameron's parents and Mom and Dad? Tell them what's happening. We'll try and stall Brett and his gang!"

"Right," James said with a firm nod. He headed back into the crush.

Mandy and Cameron pushed their way through the crowd and burst out of the front door. The men were climbing into the big green van.

"Stop," Mandy cried out, grabbing Brett McCatter's sleeve. "You can't shoot the wolves. They're young. They haven't done any harm."

"Let go of me!" McCatter growled, wrenching his sleeve from Mandy's grasp and sending her sprawling back against Cameron. "What do you know about it, anyway? I won't have a girl telling *me* what to do," he sneered.

"Huh," she snorted, running to the back of the van and looking in. She could see at least three guns fixed to the side of the van. "He must have planned this,

Cameron," she said, her voice stiff with anger. "We've got to stop him."

"How can we?" Cameron asked as the door slammed shut. "They're leaving now."

James came rushing up to them as the van roared into life and began to drive off.

"I can't find *any* of your parents," he gasped, out of breath. "I looked everywhere. Someone said that Mr. Mudie was showing your mom and dad around. They could be anywhere."

"OK. We'll have to do it without them," decided Mandy. She turned to Cameron. "Is there any way we can get to the park before McCatter?"

"Yes, through the woods — do you remember where Blackie was hurt?" Cameron said. Then he frowned. "Why?"

"Because *we've* got to get there first," she said, starting forward. "We've *got* to find the wolves. Come on!"

Eight

"Stop, Mandy!" James protested. "We can't go running around in the woods when there are men with guns there!"

"But we *have* to go," Mandy said impatiently. "If we get there first, they can't go around shooting the wolves."

"I'd like to believe that," Cameron said. "But Brett McCatter can be nasty. He wasn't even invited tonight. He just crashed the party and Dad felt it would be bad manners to turn him away."

"Mandy, we can't go without telling your parents. We promised not to go into the woods," James said.

"Right, I'll look for them," she agreed. "James, if you get our coats, I'll find Mom and Dad. Meet you back here."

"You've only got a couple of minutes, Mandy," Cameron warned her. "After that, it will be too late to beat the van to the wildlife park."

Mandy sped up the steps and scanned the Great Hall. Her parents were nowhere to be seen. Time was running out for the wolves. She made a snap decision and, picking up a white paper napkin, she ran over to Donald.

"Have you got a pen?" she asked quickly.

The storekeeper reached in his inside pocket and pulled one out. "Can we help?" he said kindly. "Are you worried about the wolves?"

Mandy nodded. "Yes," she said, scribbling a note on the napkin.

Gone to the park to look for the wolves. Couldn't find you. Don't worry — we'll be careful. Love, Mandy.

She handed back the pen and folded the paper napkin. "Could you give this to my parents, please?" she asked Donald and his wife. Their name is Hope — I think they're with Angus." Thrusting the note into his hand, she dashed out the front door.

"Let's go!" Mandy shouted to James and Cameron as she flew down the steps. James passed her coat to her and she quickly put it on.

"What did your parents say?" James quizzed her as they ran. "I thought they'd come with us. Are they driving to the wildlife park?"

"I couldn't find them, actually," Mandy said breathlessly. Cameron was running really quickly.

"What?" James exclaimed, skidding to a halt. "I don't believe it!"

"I did leave them a note," Mandy answered. "They'll understand that we don't have any choice. We *can't* let the wolves get killed! Let's get a move on!" she said, forging ahead.

When James caught up with her, she was standing above a brook, while Cameron clambered down the bank below them.

"This is a shortcut to the park, but be careful," he called. "It's very slippery because the mud has frozen over."

Mandy inched her way down the steep bank, clutching at plants and bushes to stop herself from sliding out of control. At the bottom, she and Cameron waited for James, before they all waded across the stream.

"Ah," Mandy gasped. "It's freezing!" Her new pants were wet up to her knees. Her best shoes were soaked and covered with mud.

They climbed up the bank on the other side. Mandy's

fingers were so cold that they hurt. Her shoes were making blisters. But none of that mattered. The important thing was to get to the wolves before the hunting party.

The path they were following had narrowed so they had to run in single file. Mandy felt her pants catch on a bramble and rip. Cameron's knee socks were around his ankles, and James's dark pants were covered with mud.

Suddenly, there was a loud shriek as a startled bird flew into the air. Instantly, Mandy remembered the sound of the trap clanging shut.

"Cameron, slow down," she panted as he tore along in front of her. "Don't forget that there could be traps set around here."

"We're nearly at the perimeter fence between the estate and the wildlife park," Cameron said softly, slowing to a walk and pointing ahead of them. "Look, there it is."

"But there's something wrong," James said, pushing his glasses firmly onto his nose. "It's not standing up straight."

"It's a hole — there's a big hole!" Mandy said, horrified as they reached it. "In both fences. No wonder the wolves got out."

"The fences have been cut!" James said. "Look at the edges."

"They used bolt cutters," Cameron observed bitterly. "They'll cut through *anything*."

"Let's start searching the woods," Mandy said, her mouth set in a grim line. "It's more important than ever that we find the young wolves. McCatter obviously means to shoot them, no matter what."

"Mandy, look!" Cameron clutched her arm as she started to run. She turned swiftly and looked in the direction he was pointing. Lights were moving toward them. And they were getting closer.

"Headlights!" she muttered darkly. Mandy felt a shiver of fear. McCatter's gang was getting very close. "Come on!" she shouted. "We've got to find them first!"

Spreading out, but still keeping one another in view, they began walking slowly into the darkest parts of the woods. Mandy looked back over her shoulder. The lights had stopped moving. As she watched, they went out completely. The hunters had arrived.

Nine

Mandy started forward again. James was on her left and Cameron to her right. In the wintry night, hardly anything moved. An owl flew above their heads and peered down inquisitively at them. Suddenly, Mandy stopped and waited. The other two drew nearer to her.

"Look ahead," she whispered. "I'm sure I saw movement — it was up there by the oak tree." They crept on as silently as they could. Mandy felt nervous, but she *had* to keep calm. She mustn't frighten the wolves!

Whaaaaarrr! Something gave a loud, angry wail right in front of them. Mandy clutched her throat with shock and stood rigid.

113

Suddenly, a snarling creature with a blunt-ended tail shot up a tree. It stopped on a branch with its hackles raised, flashing its eyes at Mandy. It looked so furious that, for one awful moment, Mandy thought it was going to launch itself straight at her head.

"It's a wildcat," Cameron whispered. "They're very, very dangerous. Even the kittens are fierce."

Under normal circumstances, nothing could have dragged Mandy from the wildcat, but tonight she had a more important task. Continuing through the forest, they disturbed several rabbits and one disgruntled weasel. Mandy glanced over her shoulder every few seconds. Occasionally, she saw the flicker of a light, but nothing more. She waited for the boom of a gunshot but didn't hear a sound.

Leading the way, Mandy struggled through a huge bramble patch. She felt the thorns scratching at her legs and tugging at her clothes. Bitter tears of frustration welled up in her eyes. How could they have been so foolish? They had *no* chance of finding the wolves in such a large forest.

At long last, she freed herself from the brambles. Wiping her face with a sleeve, she peered into the darkness. And two pairs of yellow eyes stared back at her.

It was the wolves!

Holding their tails in the air, the young wolves

growled and bared their fangs. The three searchers stood very still. The wolves wouldn't let Mandy get any closer. She could hardly believe these were the same animals that she had stroked and played with yesterday.

"We're here to help you," Mandy said softly at last. "You have to let us." Almost as if they were reassured by her voice, the wolves trotted a few paces away, then turned to watch her, ears pricked. But when Mandy moved toward them, they ran off again.

"Oh, no," she groaned to James and Cameron. "Now they want to play games. We'll have to follow them — we can't lose them now!"

Sprinting after the wolves and trying desperately to keep them in sight, Mandy lost all sense of direction. But, at last, they slowed down.

"Where are we?" Mandy asked Cameron when he and James caught up.

"We're still on estate land, but we've moved away from the park," Cameron answered. "That's good for the wolves. I doubt that McCatter will stray too far from the wildlife park." But as he said it, James pointed at the wolves.

"Look," he urged. "I think they've spotted something."

The young wolves had stopped to sniff the ground. Mandy, James, and Cameron stood still, watching.

Then, to their horror, the wolves turned back toward the park. There was nothing they could do except follow them. Mandy felt her heart sink as the wolves began loping through the woods, so quickly and silently that they could only just keep them in sight. They were heading straight into danger!

"They're slowing down." James was panting. "Look, there's something moving up ahead."

Mandy quickly stopped and crept closer to the wolves. Now she could see the shape of a rabbit up ahead. "They're hunting," she said. "They can't miss from that distance." But the wolves were young and this was their first hunt. They were so excited that they began wagging their tails. Immediately, the rabbit saw them. In a flash, it sprang up and ran into a burrow. The wolves stood pawing at the ground.

"Aren't they funny!" Mandy could hardly hold in her laughter.

"Let's see if we can get closer to them," said James.

At the burrow, the wolves were still busily trying to make the rabbit come out. The black wolf barked with frustration.

Mandy gasped. "Don't," she called to them. "Don't let the hunters know where you are."

The wolves stared across at Mandy. To her dismay, they pricked up their ears and trotted away once more.

"Not again!" she said, and went after them. Then she stopped so abruptly that James almost crashed into her.

Mandy felt every sense in her body go on red alert. Ahead of the wolves, half-buried in the ground, was the glint of metal — a trap.

But, to her immense relief, the wolves stopped before they reached the trap. Then they turned and watched the three followers.

"What's wrong?" James asked softly.

"There." Mandy nodded toward the wolves. "Look behind them, at the bottom of the tree."

"It's a trap!" Cameron declared, his voice grim. "You can just see the plate in the middle."

"We have to draw them away from it," Mandy said. "Maybe if we back off, they might follow."

"It's worth a try," said James.

Carefully they stepped backward until there was more space between them and the wolves.

"Please," Mandy begged under her breath. "Please come to us. Don't go the other way. It's *so* dangerous."

"Come!" she heard Cameron mutter. "Come here."

But the wolves seemed to have lost interest in them. Now that Mandy wouldn't play games, they began to wander off. *What else can we do?* she muttered to herself. She thought for a moment. "What if we approach them from the opposite direction?" she whispered to the others. "Then they might move *away* from the wildlife park. We've been chasing them toward it!"

"I'll go," James offered.

Then, before James could move, Cameron put a hand on his arm. "I think it's too late. Look!"

The wobbling light of flashlights was coming straight for them.

"Maybe it's Mom and Dad," Mandy suggested.

Cameron shook his head. "I don't think so. They'd call out, wouldn't they?"

Mandy nodded. "It's McCatter," she said in a miserable voice. She felt desperate. And then she felt a strange sensation pricking at the back of her neck. The young wolves began jumping around and acting skittishly. Then they stopped very still — it was as if their fur was standing on end.

"They must have heard the hunters," Cameron said quietly.

Mandy suddenly sensed something close by — she could tell that the wolves felt it, too. A cloud blocked out the moon, casting the forest in darkness. In vain, they craned forward to see the wolves, but the cloud passed and moonlight shone down again.

Between the trap and the wolves stood a huge animal.

"Where did *that* come from?" said Cameron in amazement.

Mandy didn't answer. Her eyes were locked onto those of the old wolf. It met her gaze for a few seconds and then looked away toward the young wolves, baring its teeth. Instantly, they flattened their ears and tucked their tails between their legs. They began to creep toward it, keeping their bodies low to the ground. But the old wolf bared its fangs at them again, and the young wolves veered off toward Mandy.

She stepped forward. The young wolves turned and looked back at the old wolf, then went up to Mandy and stood waiting. Tears stung her eyes as she looked at the old wolf. "I'll keep them safe," she whispered.

"Mandy," she heard James call softly. "Hurry up — the gang's coming."

She grabbed the young gray wolf by its thick scruff, gesturing to James to hold the other, and they all crouched down as low as they could behind some thornbushes. The old gray wolf was standing its ground, apparently quite unconcerned that the hunters were approaching.

Go away! Mandy willed the old wolf to go, but still he stood there.

The light from the flashlights was very close now, and they could make out figures coming through the woods.

"They're here," Mandy said, clutching the young wolf's scruff.

"Will you look at that?" They heard Brett McCatter laugh. "It's just waiting for us."

"But that's not a young wolf," one of the other hunters said.

"That wolf is much older," they heard another man say in a nervous voice. "And a big one at that. Where did it come from, McCatter?"

"Who cares?" McCatter cut in. "It's a wolf — and the only safe wolf is a dead one."

Booooom! A single shot rang out, deafeningly loud in the still night air.

The old wolf stood watching the hunters, not moving a muscle.

"How could I have missed it?" Brett McCatter's voice was now tense and panicky. "Fire!" he shouted. "Everyone, fire!"

Shots rang out from the guns and echoed throughout the woods.

When the firing had stopped, Mandy could hardly bear to look.

"Why doesn't it fall?" said a frantic voice. "We've peppered it with enough lead to kill *twenty* wolves."

To Mandy's amazement, the old wolf was still standing there, motionless. It had raised its hackles, making it look even bigger, and its yellow eyes seemed to glow in the darkness. Somehow, it didn't look old anymore.

"We couldn't have missed it, not at that range," another of the men said, his voice trembling with fear.

"I'm going! I don't want to be involved with this," shouted someone else, throwing down his gun.

Mandy could see that their faces were chalk-white in the moonlight as they ran away, leaving McCatter alone. He stared at the wolf as if he were hypnotized. The old wolf raised its head, looked up at the sky, and started to howl. At once, the air was filled with the deafening sound of hundreds of wolves howling! Mandy shivered uncontrollably.

Then, abruptly, the sound stopped. Brett McCatter backed away with a look of sheer terror as the old wolf began to walk slowly toward him — its eyes blazing.

McCatter stood rigid, unable to look away, unable to turn and run after his companions. His knees trembled, and the gun fell from his grasp onto the ground. The old wolf was now only five yards away from McCatter, advancing ever closer.

Mandy stood watching, holding tight to the young wolf.

"Will the wolf attack?" James asked her.

"I don't know," murmured Mandy.

With a cry, McCatter broke free from the huge animal's hypnotic gaze. Then he turned and ran for his life. He crashed recklessly through the undergrowth, stumbling headlong into a ditch, to emerge seconds later covered in mud. Then he was up and running again.

The old wolf watched calmly as McCatter disappeared among the trees. Then it turned to face Mandy. She met the old wolf's eyes, somehow knowing that this would be the last time that she'd see it. The old wolf shifted its gaze to the young wolves.

Mandy knelt down and put an arm around each animal. "Trust me," she said, looking up.

But the old wolf had melted away among the trees.

Ten

They were silent as they walked back to Cameron's house. The young wolves also seemed subdued. It had been a strange time for them all. They were almost home when they saw the lights of flashlights coming toward them. For a second, Mandy worried that it might be the gang, but something told her that they would be much too scared to come back.

"Mandy! James!" Dr. Adam's voice thundered out.

"Cameron, is that you?" It was Angus Mudie.

"Over here, Dad!" Mandy called, exchanging nervous glances with James and Cameron. "We've got the wolves with us — they're safe."

"Mandy Hope, you've gone too far this time!" Dr. Adam said in an angry voice as he hurried over. "Your note gave us a terrible shock. Then we heard gunshots! We couldn't imagine *what* was happening!"

"We didn't have any choice. There wasn't enough time, Dad," Mandy explained, her voice flustered. "The gang had already left and I *did* look for you, honestly."

"We only got there in the nick of time, Dr. Adam," Cameron said. "McCatter wanted to kill the wolves."

"That's all very well, Cameron," Dr. Adam said. "But there were guns involved!" He put his hands on his hips and stared at them. "And what about your promise, Mandy?"

Mandy looked up at her dad's face. "I'm really sorry, Dad," she said, looking down at the ground, realizing what a great risk they'd taken. "I didn't mean to make you worry, but the wolves were in such danger . . ."

". . . that you had to act first and think later," said Dr. Adam, finishing the sentence for her. "But you're all safe and sound, so I suppose that's all that really matters," he said, relenting and giving Mandy a hug.

"I must admit that without you, these young wolves would almost certainly be dead," Angus Mudie said with a grudging smile. "Officer Farish has gone after McCatter and his gang," he told them. "He's promised to let us know as soon as he catches them."

"What do we do about the wolves?" Cameron asked his father.

"Duncan and Sally are on their way," Angus told them. "They were too late getting back to come to the party, so they went straight home. They were horrified to find that the wolves had left the park. They telephoned, and I told them we were just going out to search for you."

Duncan and Sally were in the driveway, talking anxiously to Pat Mudie and Emily Hope, when they returned. Immediately, Mandy's mom and Mrs. Mudie came flying down the steps toward the bedraggled group.

"Mandy, you gave us such a scare! I was horribly worried when I heard the shots," Dr. Emily said, hugging her daughter tightly.

Mrs. Mudie sighed and put an arm around Cameron. "Whatever were you thinking, running off like that?"

"They were going to shoot the wolves, Mom," Cameron said. "We had to stop them."

"And you did, didn't you?" Mrs. Mudie said with a trace of pride in her voice. "But look at the condition you are all in!" she said. "You must be frozen. I'll go and make everyone a nice hot drink."

"Not for us, Pat," Sally called after her. She was putting leashes on the wolves. "I can't imagine how they got out, Mandy, but you found them *and* made them come with you. How on earth did you manage it?"

"We had a little help from — " Mandy stopped mid-sentence. Then, seeing Sally's puzzled look, she hurriedly added, "Someone cut a big hole in the fence — *that's* how they got out."

"Someone *wanted* them to get out," James said darkly.

"Cut a hole in the fence?" Duncan repeated, stomping angrily around the van. "That's a criminal offense — I'll make sure that the police know about this!" Then he looked toward the two wolves and sighed. "We'd better get these two home now," he said, laying a blanket in the back of the van.

Mandy helped Sally lead the wolves over to the van. They looked up at her as she stroked them both, then held their heads close. "I don't know who he was, but he saved your lives *twice* tonight," she whispered to them, suddenly realizing that it was very quiet behind her. As she turned around, she saw that everyone was staring at her.

"You have a rare gift with animals, Mandy," Angus Mudie said thoughtfully. "A rare gift indeed."

"You certainly get along with these two," agreed Duncan, coaxing the wolves into the van and closing the doors. "Thank you *all* for your help tonight," he added.

As they trooped inside, James nudged Mandy. "What are you going to say about the old wolf?"

"I don't know yet," she replied.

"Here we are," Pat Mudie announced, coming out of the kitchen. "Hot fruit punch to warm you up."

"Just the thing, Pat," Dr. Adam said, smiling. "We've all had quite a shock tonight. By the way, James . . ." He paused as James looked over at him. "It did cross my mind what I would say to your parents, if anything had happened to you out there."

James blushed.

"As it is, we'll have to explain how you managed to ruin your best pants!" said Dr. Adam, trying to smother a grin.

But before anyone could say anything, there was a tap on the door. It was Officer Farish. Mrs. Mudie gave him a hot fruit punch, and they all sat around waiting expectantly for his news.

"Thank you, Pat," Officer Farish said, taking a sip of the punch. "Now, I certainly don't wish to encourage such reckless behavior, but I have to admit that between you" — he looked from Mandy and James to Cameron — "you did a pretty good night's work."

Mandy grinned. "Did you catch McCatter and the others?"

"Thanks to you, I certainly did!" Officer Farish explained. "It turns out that McCatter planned this as soon as the wolves arrived. The party gave him the opportunity he needed. Half the neighborhood was here, and everyone knew that Duncan and Sally would be away. The coast was clear. McCatter cut the fences, then came to the party, leaving Gary Kemp to raise the alarm. Incidentally, he works for McCatter on the farm."

"So McCatter had it all planned," said Dr. Adam. "Right down to the last detail."

"Almost. But he couldn't have known that these youngsters would get the wolves to safety before he was even on the scene," Officer Farish said with a chuckle.

"They were shooting at — " Cameron burst out, but was quickly silenced by a look from Mandy. "Aren't you going to arrest them?" he continued.

"They're all down at the station now, waiting to be charged," Officer Farish said. "When I found him, McCatter was on his knees, shaking from head to toe. He was babbling incoherently about haunted woods, ghostly wolves, and all sorts of strange things. He says that he'll never set foot in the woods again, not as long as he lives!"

"Haunted woods?" Angus Mudie declared. "Ghosts? Nonsense! I've walked in those woods for years and I've never seen anything out of the ordinary. The man's gone crazy."

Mandy, James, and Cameron looked at one another knowingly.

Officer Farish spotted the exchange of glances. "Did any of you see anything suspicious or dangerous in the woods this evening?" he asked, looking Mandy straight in the eye.

"No," Mandy replied honestly. As far as she was concerned, there was nothing suspicious or dangerous about the old wolf. "McCatter and his gang were the only dangerous things."

"Well, then," Officer Farish said, standing up and putting on his cap. "I'll go and see Duncan in the morning. He'll have charges of his own to add, no doubt. McCatter won't forget *this* party in a hurry!"

Mandy turned to Cameron when the policeman had left the room. "Did you find the picture of the wolf that you were telling us about?" she asked.

"I haven't told Mom that it's missing yet," Cameron replied.

"What's missing?" Mrs. Mudie asked.

"The portrait of Fiona's wolf," Cameron said. "I showed Mandy and James the sketchbook, and it wasn't there."

"Of course it's there, Cameron." Mrs. Mudie smiled. "Where else would it be? It's been there for hundreds of years — it's hardly likely to be missing on its own now, is it?"

"Honestly, Mom, it *wasn't* there," said Cameron, looking at Mandy and James for confirmation. "Was it?"

"It wasn't, Mrs. Mudie," Mandy agreed. "There was just a blank page."

"A blank page?" Mrs. Mudie looked puzzled. "Angus, could you get the book down, please? Let's sort this out."

"Whose sketchbook?" Dr. Emily asked.

"Fiona was a young girl who was sent here to recover from an illness in the eighteenth century," Angus Mudie explained, passing the box to his wife, who told the rest of the story.

"Fiona was distraught when she found out that the wolf was dead," Mrs. Mudie concluded a few moments later. "Her parents gave her this sketchbook, and she drew all of these beautiful pictures." Cameron's mom turned the delicate pages carefully.

"They're exquisite," Dr. Emily said. "Is that Fiona?"

Mandy leaned closer as Mrs. Mudie nodded, before turning the page. "Here we are," she said, holding it up and smiling at them. "Here's the wolf portrait. I *knew* it wasn't missing."

Mandy took a breath and felt her eyes widening. Staring back at her was the old wolf.

"And these marks are where Fiona shed tears as she drew it," Mandy heard Mrs. Mudie say, but it sounded as if she were a long way away.

Somehow, Mandy thought, *the old wolf knew that the young wolves were in danger. It didn't want them to be shot, as it had been, and it knew they'd need our help.* She dragged her gaze away and looked at James and Cameron. They both looked stunned, too.

"Mandy, look at its eyes," Dr. Emily said. "She's drawn them beautifully. What a strange expression . . ."

Mandy stared at the portrait. It was all in black and white, but she knew that the old wolf's eyes were a

glowing yellow. Its eyes had been so sad when she had first seen it at the window. But now they were very different.

"I know exactly what its expression means," Mandy said positively. "It looks proud!" She grinned at them all. "The old gray wolf looks proud."

HAUNTINGS

Look for the next
Animal Ark™ Hauntings book:

HOUND ON THE HEATH

Mandy was starting to think that they were venturing too far from camp, when James suddenly gasped.

"Look! Mandy!"

Ahead of them, they could see the blackened, ruined walls of a small building. Ivy-covered and broken, the toppled stones lay in heaps across the old foundation. Only the remains of a door frame stood upright, still fixed to the floor. Dried leaves rustled in a swirl of wind and rose spookily, before settling with a sigh.

James swiveled the flashlight, picking out the cavernous mouth of an ancient fireplace. "It's in ruins," he whispered in awe. "It must be ages since anyone lived here."

A fierce gust of wind rushed at the house, and the door frame swayed and groaned under the onslaught. There was the sound of frantically fluttering wings. A hundred or more flapping creatures erupted from the crumbling walls of the cottage. They burst up into the night sky, giving off a high, thin wail as they swooped and dived for cover.

Mandy gasped and cowered in shock.

"Bats!" said James, who had ducked his head and was keeping it low. "We must have disturbed a whole colony of them!"

Mandy breathed a sigh of relief and stood up again. Her legs still felt shaky.

The ruin was deserted — and the howling seemed to have stopped. Blackie stood between them, as close as he could get to the reassuring safety of the people he loved. His ears were lying flat on his head, and his tail was tucked tightly between his legs.

"It's stopped," James whispered, his voice strained with nerves. "Look, we'd better turn back."

Suddenly, the bruised darkness of the night was split by a flash of white light. It was a great flash of lightning, illuminating the moor and the ruined house. Mandy clutched again at James and in that terrifying second, standing among the ruins, they saw it.

It was the creature that everyone had told them about.

Into the arc of light cast by James's trembling flashlight beam, stepped a thin and elegant greyhound.

Mandy's eyes widened in surprise. The dog was the palest gray — almost white. On its sculptured face was the saddest expression Mandy had ever seen. "Oh, James!" she murmured. "Poor dog!"

Mandy felt that James was squeezing her arm a little harder than he intended. His eyes were fixed on the dog. Blackie had dropped back, his head drooping. And, as they watched, the greyhound in the ruins lifted its head and howled. It was a bloodcurdling moan that sent shivers running down Mandy's back to the very base of her spine.